Joy stood and moved behind her sister then started massaging her shoulders.

"You could have a real problem brewing, you know. You're playing kissy-face with a semi-engaged man. Boy, would the elder Sheltons go into shock if they knew about that!"

"It was a simple, sympathetic kiss, Joy. Nothing more."

"Yeah," her sister said, her brow raised. "He probably kisses all his patients like that."

Catherine bent over and lowered her head. Her sister's kneading felt good. She hadn't realized how tight her neck and shoulder muscles had become. Spending eight hours a day at the computer didn't help either.

"He claims the marriage thing is her idea. Hers and his parents'. He says he's not ready for marriage. Who knows if he's telling the truth?"

Joy pressed her thumbs into her sister's neck muscles. "You think he'd lie to you?"

Catherine turned to face her sister. "Why not? I'm lying to him, aren't I?"

JOYCE LIVINGSTON has done many things in her life (in addition to being a wife, mother of six, and grandmother to oodles of grandkids, all of whom she loves dearly). From being a television broadcaster for eighteen years, to lecturing and teaching on quilting and sewing, to writing magazine articles on a variety of subjects. She's danced with Lawrence Welk, ice-skated with a chimpanzee, had bottles broken over her head by stuntmen, interviewed hundreds of celebrities and controversial figures, and done many other interesting and unusual things. But now, when she isn't off traveling to wonderful and exotic places as a part-time tour escort, her days are spent sitting in front of her computer, creating stories. She feels her writing is a ministry and a calling from God, and she hopes her readers will be touched and uplifted by what she writes. Joyce loves to hear from her readers and invites you to visit her on the Internet at: www.joycelivingston.com

Books by Joyce Livingston

HEARTSONG PRESENTS
HP353—Ice Castle
HP382—The Bride Wore Boots
HP437—Northern Exposure
HP516—Lucy's Quilt
HP521—Be My Valentine
HP546—Love is Kind
HP566—The Baby Quilt

The Birthday Wish

Joyce Livingston

Heartsong Presents

To my sister-in-law, Ruth Houston of Milwaukee, Oregon. A school-teacher for many years, Ruth has been an inspiration and an encouragement to the hundreds of young people who have been fortunate enough to attend her classes. Although she is in her nineties now, and living in a care-home, she has a ready smile for everyone with whom she comes in contact and is still able to quote the many Bible verses she learned over the years. I love you, Ruth. You are indeed a blessing.

A note from the Author:
I love to hear from my readers! You may correspond with me by writing:

> **Joyce Livingston**
> **Author Relations**
> **PO Box 719**
> **Uhrichsville, OH 44683**

ISBN 1-58660-920-3

THE BIRTHDAY WISH

Our mission is to publish and distribute inspirational products offering exceptional value and biblical encouragement to the masses.

All of the characters and events in this book are fictitious. Any resemblance to actual persons, living or dead, or to actual events is purely coincidental.

PRINTED IN THE U.S.A.

one

"Jo—Jonah? What're you doing here?" Catherine Barton stared at the handsome, well-dressed man standing on the other side of the storm door. Her stomach churned, and a nauseous feeling swept over her. Bittersweet memories crowded her thoughts, memories she'd struggled hard to bury for ten long years.

His hand rested on the door handle, and he peered through the double pane of insulated glass that separated them, a slight smile on his face. "Aren't you going to invite me in?"

She gulped hard. She'd heard rumors that Jonah Shelton might be coming back to Dallas, but she'd never expected him to come looking for her. She ventured a quick glance in the hall mirror and tugged at her hair. Why hadn't she taken time to apply fresh lipstick after she'd consumed that hurried sandwich at her desk? Looking less than one's best was a hazard of running a home-based business. Her fingers found the small lever on the lock, and she pushed the door open with trepidation. "Uh. . .sure. I guess. Co—come on in."

"I felt a little uneasy about coming. I wasn't sure if I'd be welcome, but I had to see you."

The same tall, stately Jonah Shelton she'd known as a youth brushed past her and made his way into her living room, the masculine scent of his aftershave lingering behind him. She blinked hard and took a deep breath as she felt an uncertain twang on her heart strings. She'd thought him handsome as a teenager, but the man standing before her was drop-dead gorgeous. His pale blue eyes were even bluer than she remembered, and they were focused on her.

"You're as pretty as ever. Did you know it's been a decade since I've seen you?" He stood facing her, his broad hands resting on her shoulders, and grinned.

She wondered if he felt as uneasy in her presence as she felt in his. "Ten years, nine months, and two weeks to be exact."

Her hasty retort slipped out before she could stop it.

He shook his hands free and raised a questioning brow. "I hope you're not marking X's on a calendar."

Catherine turned away, determined to avoid eye contact with this man who'd meant so much to her. Even now, after all this time, just the mere sight of him sent shivers up her spine. "No, of course, not, but I'll never—"

"Never forget what my parents did to us? Having our marriage annulled after our one night together, since we were nothing more than"—he took a deep breath—"than teenagers who thought they were in love, and. . ." He lowered his head and let the rest of his words drift off.

·Thought they were in love? she wanted to cry out to him. Did he need to be reminded of what had happened the last time they'd been together?

"I hate to say this because I know it will upset you, but we probably shouldn't have gotten married, Cat. I think we both knew my parents would never allow our marriage to continue."

Shapeless echoes of silence hung heavily in the room while two people who'd known each other so well stared at one another as if they were no more than strangers.

Several times Jonah started to speak again, but his voice seemed to fail him.

Her eyes swept his face, searching for the reason for his being there. Why doesn't he just go away and leave me alone?

"The whole thing wasn't fair to you, Cat. I should never have put you in that position." He ducked his head and rotated his fingers and thumb across the dark trace that had barely begun to accumulate on his chin. "I'll live with that guilt for the rest of my life. I–I never meant to hurt you, Cat. I had to come and tell you." He was obviously struggling for words, but his voice was kind and gentle as he reached out and cupped her shoulder. This time, although she tried to move away, he held on and wouldn't allow it. "I should've been strong enough to stand up to them. I realized that too late. Even after all this time I can see the hatred in your eyes, Cat. Hatred I deserve, and I'm here to apologize. I'm a changed man now. Please give me a chance to make things right."

She fought to gain control over the wide gamut of emotions she was certain displayed themselves on her face. The night his parents had come to the tiny motel room they'd rented for their honeymoon and snatched her new husband away had changed her life forever.

"Did you ever tell them we. . . ?" She couldn't bring herself to say the words. She watched as his Adam's apple rose and fell with an awkward swallow.

"No—I couldn't bring myself to do it. What went on between the two of us was much too personal."

After a bit of silence she bowed her head and responded in a mere whisper. "I didn't think you would."

"I–I couldn't," he confessed, his voice barely audible.

She let out a long, slow sigh.

"I'm sure they guessed, but they never brought it up."

"You hurt me, Jonah. I thought our love was real. Then, only hours after we stood before that justice of the peace and pledged our lives to one another, you let your parents lead you off like a mere child, out of my life, without even a look back."

"I wanted to stay—honest, I did." His hand reached for hers, but she withdrew it. "I realize now what a coward I was. But what they said made sense—at the time."

"Made sense?" She hurled the words at him as if they were darts and he was the bull's-eye. "How easily you were convinced! Their feeble explanations made no sense to me at all.

You should've had the decency to defend our love and our marriage. Instead you left me there alone on our wedding night. How could you?"

From the wounded expression on his face she could see her words had hit the bull's-eye—right smack in the center.

"I tried to call you that night, after my parents went to bed, but I guess you didn't stay at the motel once we'd left. I let the phone ring and ring, but either you'd gone to your parents' house or you didn't want to talk to me. I never knew which."

"What were you going to say? That your socialite parents were right? That you had no business marrying beneath you?"

"You make me sound pretty callous." Again he extended his hand, but she took another step backward, refusing to let him touch her.

He dropped his hand and held it behind his back. "You have every right to be upset with me. I was callous. I admit it, and I'm begging for your forgiveness. Please don't shut me out!"

"You could have tried to find me," she said curtly.

"You weren't at the motel!"

"You could've phoned my parents' house." She folded her arms across her chest with pent-up indignation. "You certainly knew the number! You'd called it often enough when we were dating."

"I–I wanted to, but it was late, and I was afraid the call would upset your parents when I couldn't find you. So I–I didn't do anything but lie awake in my own bed and feel like a heel." He gave her a sheepish grin she interpreted as guilt. "I–I wasn't sure if you had any money for a taxi, or—"

Her eyes narrowed. "So you went merrily on your way with your life and forgot about me?"

"No!" he shot back. "It wasn't that way at all! I–I didn't forget about you, but what could I do? I was leaving for college the next day. When I finally got hold of your mom and she said you didn't want to talk to me—well, I just quit trying to reach you. I figured you hated me for everything and wanted me to stay out of your life."

"I only hated what you did to me, Jonah. Not you!"

He stared at her uneasily. "I should've called you from college, but it seemed so awkward, talking to you on the phone. I felt as if I owed it to you to talk with you in person. That's—that's why I put it off until Christmas. I felt like a traitor for what my parents and I had done to you."

A snappy retort reached her lips, but she clamped down on the words before they escaped.

"It wasn't until I went off to college and was separated from my parents and out from under their domination that I realized what a wimp I'd been. I've wanted to apologize, to set things straight, and—"

"Please, either leave, or let's change the subject." She rubbed her temples and turned away. "I'm getting a headache, and I really don't want to talk about this anymore. What's done is done. Our lives as Mr. and Mrs. Jonah Shelton ended that night. It's no big deal I've recovered, and I'm sure you have, too." She hoped she sounded convincing.

"Fine with me." He shrugged as he seated himself on her sofa. "I never wanted this to turn into an argument."

She preferred that he leave, but she watched with interest as he stuck his long legs out in front of him and leaned back into the plump cushions.

"So, Cat, how've you been all these years? I've wondered about you so many times. How you were. What you were doing."

How've I been? He waltzes back into my life after all these years and wants to know how I've been and what I've been doing? She balled her fingers and fought to stuff the hurt and anger back into the permanently carved-out recesses of her mind. He was right. No sense arguing about the reasons for their annulled marriage now. Not after all this time.

"Fine, I guess," she mumbled, as hurt as ever, despite her resolve. She nibbled at her lower lip, wishing he'd simply disappear and she could get on with her life. There was so much he didn't know. Events he hadn't even known about. Changes in her life that may not have happened, if. . . But they did happen, and because of them she would never be the same.

"Good. Glad to hear it. By the way, how's your sister?" He stopped, then lifted his brow. "You aren't still holding a grudge after all these years, are you, Cat? It's not like you."

How do you know what I'm like? You haven't bothered to check on me for over a decade. I could've died for all you care. She clasped her hands together to keep them from shaking. "Jo—Joy's fine. I see her nearly every day. Her apartment is just down the block."

"And. . .the grudge?" he asked, his chin jutting forward slightly. "What about that?"
. "I wouldn't exactly call it a grudge. A broken heart would describe it better."

His face softened. "Honest, Cat. I never meant to hurt you. But we were so young and naïve—"

"And in love!" she cut in. "At least I was. I thought you were, too, or I never would have let—"

"Let's be honest with one another. We both knew better than to run off and get married. You knew my parents had warned me time and time again to—"

"To stay away from me? Is that what you were going to say? The poor little girl from the wrong part of town?" She felt the heat rising to her cheeks again, but she was angry. Still. Angry at him for deserting her, angry at herself for not getting over him, and angry at how difficult it was to say the words she'd promised herself she'd say if she ever came face-to-face with him again.

Jonah blanched. "They were only concerned about my future."

"That well-planned future didn't include me, did it? Be honest, Jonah. You never were much good at lying." She swallowed hard, still having difficulty getting the words out. "You knew your parents would have our marriage annulled if we went through with it, didn't you?"

His hand moved to cover hers, but she withdrew it and linked her fingers together.

"No, of course I didn't know! How can you say such cruel things? I knew they'd be upset and maybe demand we get a divorce later on, but annulment never entered my head. I was as shocked as you were when they showed up that night!"

"Then why, Jonah? Why did you leave with them?"

"Because they convinced me it was the right thing to do! For both of us! They thought it was puppy love, Catherine. We were still in our teens!"

It was all she could do to keep from slapping him for that comment, but she didn't. No one deserved to be slapped. Instead her heart was filled with grief. Grief for what her life might have been if they hadn't had that one evening of marriage and been torn apart.

It seemed like an eternity as they sat there staring at one another. Jonah, looking as though he wished he hadn't been so careless with his words. Catherine, nearly in tears.

Finally he spoke. "Look, Cat. It's been years. Can't we just talk like old friends—without belittling one another? I need to make things right between us. This thing has been tearing me apart all these years. I accepted Christ as my Savior a few months ago and knew I had to make things right between us."

So now you're a so-called Christian and that makes things okay? Absolves you of your wrongdoing? She wanted to jump to her feet and order him to leave, but she couldn't. The same magnetism that had drawn her to him when she was a mere girl was still drawing her, whether she liked it or not. "It's been tearing me apart, too, Jonah," she replied softly. "But I said I didn't want to talk about it."

His handsome face took on a slight smile as he gave her a quick once-over. "I like your hair long. You always kept it cut short when we were in high school. It looks good on you."

"Th—thanks."

"You're much thinner than I remember but as pretty as ever."

Again she felt like that naïve schoolgirl as his eyes scanned her from tip to toe. "Ah—thanks again," she responded nervously, her fingers going to her hair. She found it difficult to accept his compliment, but she was glad for the change of direction their conversation was taking. "I've been wearing it long for a number of years now." She bit at her lip, still struggling to regain her composure. Perhaps if she allowed him to have his say he'd leave, and she could begin the process of forgetting him all over again. "I am a bit thinner, I guess."

Her fingers plowed through her blunt-cut hair as she tugged a handful toward her face. Why had he come? Surely not just to apologize! He could have done that with a simple greeting card. The last thing she'd expected, or wanted, when she'd opened the door was Jonah on her doorstep. How did he find her? And why would he want to find her? Was his story about becoming a Christian his only reason for wanting to see her? Did he want to flaunt his newfound relationship with God in her face? Or had his conscience been bothering him?

He settled himself back into the sofa with a friendly wink. "I don't suppose you've given up coffee, have you?"

The pleasant aroma floating in from the kitchen reminded her she'd put a fresh pot on just before the doorbell rang. He must've noticed. She held back the feelings of frustration and resentment she was still harboring and pasted on a smile. "I guess you'd like a cup."

He smiled. "I could use a good cup of coffee about now."

"Black, right?"

"Black. You have a good memory."

"You bet I have a good memory," she grumbled under her breath as she made her way into the sunlit kitchen. She grabbed two mugs from the cupboard and plunked them onto the countertop with a thud. *How could I forget? I fixed dozens of cups of coffee for you during the three years we dated.* She closed her eyes and leaned against the refrigerator door, her hands covering her face as the memories, both good and bad, sought to overtake her. Could she ever put those memories aside?

Lately her life had been going well. Not that she'd forgotten about him. But at least he didn't occupy her every thought, as he had those first few months after he'd gone off to college and she'd married Jimmy on the rebound.

Rebound. What a horrible-sounding word. Surely that wasn't what she'd done to sweet, sweet Jimmy. He'd admitted he had a crush on her that first day they met at his mother's beauty shop. Though she'd never expressed any affection for him other than that of a true friend, he'd accepted her at face value and loved her, despite the love he'd known she still carried in her heart for Jonah. She smiled as she remembered the pleasant times they'd shared together. No, she hadn't married Jimmy on the rebound. If she hadn't already met and cared for Jonah, she would have been attracted to Jimmy and his gentle ways. In many ways he and Jonah were—

"Need any help?" Jonah called out from the other room.

His words brought her back to the present, and she hurried to fill the cups, quickly putting her thoughts aside. "No, coming right up."

He was walking about, checking out the room, when she returned with the two steaming cups of coffee.

"Nice place. You lived here long?"

"Th—thanks," she stammered awkwardly, handing his cup to him. She placed hers on the end table before collapsing onto the recliner, noisily propping up the foot rest. "A little over two years, I guess."

"The place looks like you." He blew into the cup and took a sip then moved toward the spinet piano that stood in the corner. "I didn't know you played."

She sucked in a deep breath and fingered the buttons on her shirt. "Not really—just always wanted a piano. My folks could never afford one when we were growing up. But then I'm sure you knew that." Did her answer sound as sarcastic to him as it did to her? She didn't mean it to. Well, maybe she did. He'd never known what it was like to want something and not be able to afford it. Whatever he wanted, he got— thanks to his rich, doting parents.

"So are you taking piano lessons?" His fingers dragged across the keys noisily.

Why didn't he finish his coffee and go? Every minute she spent with him was torture as the old rancor began to rekindle and flare. "No, I'm not," she answered simply.

He picked up a book from the piano's music rack, read the title, and put it back in its place.

Was he going to ask her why a piano book was sitting on the rack, with an assignment sheet clipped to its cover?

The room began to spin around her. The man she had loved sat down again on her sofa and took another sip of coffee. His Armani suit was out of place in her modest home.

And so was he.

"Didn't I hear you married some guy named Jimmy?"

Well, he'd finally gotten around to the one question she'd expected him to ask: Was she married? Of course, maybe someone else had told him about her marital status, and he was only making polite conversation.

"Jimmy died."

His eyes widened. "He died?"

She nodded, biting her lip. Saying those two words never got any easier. She'd loved Jimmy. Their marriage had been a good one, even though their time together had been brief. "Yes, in a motorcycle accident, not long after we were married."

His eyes darkened with sympathy as he leaned forward and gave her hand a gentle squeeze.

She froze. His touch made her hand tingle. It had been years since a man had touched her—in any way. The warmth of his hand on hers brought back an abundance of memories of their teenage times together. Wonderful times.

"I'm so sorry, Cat. I didn't know. It seems most of our old friends have lost touch with you."

She lowered her head, finding it nearly impossible to look into his deep-set blue eyes. "You couldn't have known. You were away at college." She leaned back in her chair and added, "Out of my life."

Jonah didn't respond. He just stared at her.

This was the first time she'd ever seen him without words. As a teenager he'd had an answer for everything. But now that talent seemed lost.

She wiggled uneasily in her chair. "By the way, I'd appreciate it if you didn't call me Cat." *Did I have to say that?*

He grinned at her with the sideways grin that brought out the deep dimple in his left cheek. "But I've always called you Cat. Remember? It was my pet name for you."

"I hope I was more to you than a pet," she shot back testily as she picked up her cup and stared into it, avoiding his gaze. "I'd prefer you call me Catherine. Everyone does." She hoped her words sounded free of the deep emotions that were swirling inside her, but she doubted it. Something inside her stirred each time he called her Cat. He'd given her that nickname when they were in the eighth grade, and it had stuck.

"I didn't mean any disrespect. You've always been Cat to me. The name suited you." He grinned at her again. "It still does."

She watched his dimple deepen, remembering the many

times she'd touched the tip of her finger to that very spot and teased him about it. Determined to keep her voice even, she swallowed hard and stated firmly, "You lost that right ten years ago, Jonah—when you and your parents dumped me."

"Ouch! Isn't the word dump pretty harsh?"

She straightened in the chair, folded her hands, and squared her chin. "Not in my opinion. I'd say dump is putting it mildly."

He scooted to the edge of the sofa and, after hesitating a bit, rested his hand lightly on her arm.

She pushed it away.

"Look! I didn't want to leave you like that! But my parents made it seem the only reasonable thing to do. I had college ahead of—"

"College?" Her pulse raced, and her heart pounded against her chest. "We'd already discussed how I would get a job and help support us until you graduated. We could've made it on our own, as we'd planned."

"And you could've waited for me after our marriage was annulled! Instead of rushing off and marrying Jimmy! We both did things we shouldn't have."

Her fist pounded the chair's arm with a sudden thud as she bent toward him, her gaze drilling into his. "While you went off to college and dated the campus cuties—as your parents would've insisted? Sorority college girls, whose parents were as rich as your parents? No way! I had a life to live, too. You'd already proven what a mama's boy you were and how easily you were influenced by your parents' whims and their wealth. Are you so foolish as to believe they would ever have allowed us to be married?"

He stood and, with a look of frustration, lifted his hands into the air. "Cat! We were still in our teens, with our whole lives ahead of us! We went steady all through high school and were way too serious for eighteen year olds. You were the only girl I'd ever dated! How were we supposed to make an intelligent decision about whom we would marry and spend our lives with if we'd never been with anyone else? We were babies!"

"Now you sound like your parents!" Her accusation echoed off the walls of the little room. "As I recall, those were their exact words. Did you ever grow up, Jonah? Or are you still asking Mama and Daddy's permission to live your life?" Catherine lowered her elbows to her knees and buried her face in her hands. Opening old wounds was painful.

The clock ticked loudly on the mantel of the small gas fireplace, emphasizing the silence in the room. Jonah said nothing for the moment, and Catherine felt as if she'd said too much.

Finally Jonah broke the heady silence. "Look—I'm still interested in knowing about you, Cat. That's why I tried to find you. I've wondered about you over the years. Where you were, what you were doing. If you had kids." He dropped back onto the sofa and patted the cushion beside him, his voice softening. "Come and sit by me, Cat—Catherine. I can't leave knowing you feel this animosity toward me. Surely we can be friends and have a decent conversation."

Feeling guilty for her loud outburst, she feigned a smile and cautiously moved to sit on the sofa. But she left enough space between them. She reached for her cup and took a long, slow sip to steady her nerves. "Did you ever get to med school?"

He returned the smile. "Yes, graduated, too. I'm officially a doctor. I guess you thought I'd never make it."

She leaned back, feeling a reprieve, since the subject had shifted again to more pleasant things. "Actually I never doubted you'd make it. It helps if you have parents who can pay for your education while you concentrate your energies on your studies. No doubt much easier than having a wife who works at minimum wage to pay for your schooling. And you were determined to make it." *I just can't let it go, can I?* She licked her lips nervously. "So you have your own practice now?"

He nodded, apparently ignoring her comment about a working wife. "Yes. In Denver. I bought into a partnership owned by my uncle Bert and a group of other doctors."

"Denver?"

"Yep, Denver." He smiled. "Our clinic is a kind of do-it-all-in-one-stop thing. You know, like a shopping mall for good health."

"That sounds like a practical concept." She took another sip of her now-cold coffee and watched his eyes light up as he talked about his profession. She had always thought he would make a good doctor. She hated what had happened between them, but she was glad he'd reached his long-range goal.

His face shone with excitement. "It was my idea to promote it that way. We wanted a place where people of all ages could come for their health care. We have a general practitioner, an obstetrician, a pediatrician, a surgeon, a cardiologist, a urologist, gynecologist, nutritionist, physical therapist, dentist, chiropractor"—he paused and drew in a deep breath—"and me! We even have a local pastor on call twenty-four hours a day."

She wrinkled her brows. "And you? What are you?"

"Reconstructive surgeon," he answered proudly. "I get to help my Uncle Bert put people back together. That man has years of experience behind him."

"It must be very rewarding," she observed with sincere interest as she reached to tug her hair back over her cheek. "So are you here visiting your parents?"

"Yes and no." He took another sip.

She wondered if he'd even noticed his coffee had cooled off.

"Our clinic in Denver is doing so well that we've decided to branch out. We've opened the same type of clinic in Dallas. I'm here to stay, Cat. At least until the clinic is on its feet."

If he'd hit her on the head with a brick, he couldn't have stunned her more. Knowing he'd moved away from Dallas was the main reason she had moved back. The population of

Dallas was quite large, but the possibility of running into him had still terrified her. Now here he was in her very own living room, giving her the news she'd feared most. He was back.

Jonah leaned toward her and pinched her arm lightly. "Hey, there! Cat! Did you hear me? I said I've moved back to Dallas."

She couldn't let him see how much his announcement had upset her. She struggled to keep control of her skittish emotions and her wavering voice. "Yes, I heard. Mo—more coffee?" She rose carefully and reached for his cup as his cellular phone rang. "I'll—I'll get the coffee. Go ahead and answer your phone."

From the kitchen she could hear his every word. The caller must have been a woman, probably his wife. He kept making excuses about why he hadn't called, then said he would phone later that night. From his side of the conversation it seemed obvious the woman was dissatisfied with his answers. Finally he said with agitation, "I'm visiting an old friend. I'll call you later."

Catherine walked back into the room, placed the cup of steaming coffee in his outstretched hand, and sat down on the sofa again.

He smiled. "Thanks. I never seem to get enough coffee. Guess I picked up that habit working twenty-four hours, seven days a week, at the hospital during my residency."

"Those long hours must've been tough."

He nodded. "At times, but it was worth it. I can sign that M.D. after my name now."

He had asked her some personal questions earlier, so she decided it was time she asked him some. "That your wife on the phone?"

From the way he fidgeted before answering, she wondered if things were amiss in Matrimonialville.

"No, I'm not married. At least not yet. But, according to Alexandra, I guess I'm sort of semi-engaged." He laughed nervously. "Is that a word? Semi-engaged?"

She smiled but didn't answer.

"She keeps saying she's ready to get married, but I'm not, so we're kind of marking time." He sipped at the coffee and winced when it burned his lips. "Who knows if I ever will be?"

The clock on the mantel chimed four times. Catherine jumped to her feet, desperate to end their trip down memory lane as soon as possible. "I—uh—this has been—fun, but, if you don't mind, I need to tend to some things."

His cup hit the table with a *kerplunk*. "Sure." He shrugged. "I've probably overstayed my welcome anyway. If you're busy—maybe some other time, we could—"

She shook her head vigorously. "I don't think there should be another time. You and I had our time together years ago, and it didn't work out for you. I think we should end this right now and not see one another again."

Her words were sharp and direct, but she felt she needed to say them.

Jonah stood slowly. "Look, Cat. God has been dealing with my heart, and I came here to apologize. I'd hoped you were no longer mad at me for what I allowed my parents to do. I gave you my high school years—some of the best years of my life. We—"

She nearly shouted in his face. "I remember, Jonah! I loved those years. I loved you!"

"Then why, Cat? Why are you still so angry?"

The words tumbled out unchecked. "Because that night I gave you the most precious thing a woman can offer a man!" Tears of hurt and rage spilled from her eyes.

Jonah moved awkwardly toward her, but she pushed him away.

"I would never—I mean—if I'd had any idea you'd allow your parents to break us up. . ."

He reached for her, but she stepped backward.

"I still have the wedding ring you gave me when we vowed to love and cherish each other until death. Those vows meant everything to me, but apparently they meant nothing to you!" Her tears turned to deep, uncontrolled sobs. She'd carried this burden for ten years, breaking down only in private. Never in front of anyone other than her sister. Now here she was, crying like a baby. Letting her emotions run away with her, like some sappy schoolgirl with a crush on the high school quarterback.

Jonah looked about, then tried to slip his arm around her shoulders, but she pushed him away again.

"I'm—sorry, Cat. I meant those vows, too. At the time. But I had eight years of schooling ahead of me, and—well— my parents thought it would be best for both of us if our marriage was annulled. My folks—"

"Your folks? There was never any secret about their feelings toward me, but it didn't keep you away from me in high school. You always knew how they felt about me." She dabbed at her eyes with her sleeve. "Did you ever grow up and learn to take responsibility for your own actions? Or do your parents still rule your life?"

He dropped his hands to his sides and turned away slightly, his shoulders sagging. "I'm so—sorry, Cat. I never intended to hurt you. Honest. I guess I was a cocky teenager with raging hormones. Marrying you—"

She wiped her hand across her eyes, then glanced impatiently at the clock. "I'm sorry, too. But I really have things I must do. You'd better go."

"But—well—"

"Please, Jonah. It's over."

He took a step toward the door. "Okay. I will if you want me to. But we have to talk again. Soon. There's so much I need to tell you."

"No." Her voice was firm. "The past is in the past, Jonah. As

I said before, let's leave it there. Even though we share the same memories, you and I no longer have anything in common." She walked to the door, opened it, then stepped back out of the way. "Good-bye, Jonah. Good luck with your clinic."

He reached out his hand but withdrew it when she didn't accept it. "We can't be friends?"

"I'd rather not."

His jaw squared as he strode past her, turning back only long enough to add, "If that's the way you want it, I guess I have no other choice; but I will be praying for you. Good-bye, Cat. Take care of yourself."

Before Catherine could shut the door behind him, the voice of a young girl called from the kitchen.

"Hi, Mom. I'm home!"

two

Jonah pushed his way back into the room, his eyes riveted on a young girl with long blond hair and deep blue eyes who was setting her books on the desk. " 'Mom'? You have a daughter? You never mentioned you have a daughter. I supposed you lived alone or maybe had a roommate. . . ." One glance at the girl, and his words trailed off.

Catherine gulped hard. Two minutes! If he'd left only two minutes earlier, she wouldn't have had to introduce the two of them and try to explain to her daughter who he was. "I–I guess we had so much to talk about, the subject never came up. Jonah," she said, feeling very awkward, "this is Sunni. Sunni, this is Dr. Shelton."

He stepped forward with a broad smile and reached out his hand. "Hi, Sunni. I'm an old—uh—friend of your mother's. We went to junior high and high school together."

"Hi." She smiled and grasped his hand, shaking it heartily. "Nice to meet you." She turned to her mother. "Did you bake those cookies today?"

Catherine watched Jonah's reaction to her beautiful daughter and tried to appear nonchalant. "Sure did, Honey. Chocolate chip, your favorite. Why don't you go on in the kitchen, pour yourself a glass of milk, and give them a try? Just don't eat too many and spoil your supper."

Jonah stepped past her and gave the child a friendly grin. "If you don't mind, I'd like to try some of those chocolate chip cookies myself. Your mom used to bake them for me. Chocolate chip is my favorite, too. Does she still put walnuts in them?"

Sunni's eyes widened. "My mom baked cookies for you? Neat!"

Jonah walked over to the girl. "She sure did. I loved those cookies."

Catherine forced her limbs to move. She put her arm around her daughter's shoulders. "That was a long time ago, Sunni. When Dr. Shelton left for college, we"—she hesitated, then glanced at Jonah—"lost touch."

She turned and nodded in the direction of the front door. "I'm sure a busy man like you has better things to do with his time than eat cookies in our little kitchen. Besides, I thought your fiancée was looking for you," she added coolly.

Grinning, he took a slight step toward her daughter. "I'll call her later. Anyway, she's in New York on a shopping trip with my mom." He rubbed his hands together. "Now, young lady, if it's okay with your mom, let's have those cookies."

"Mom? Is it okay with you?" Sunni eyed her mother.

Catherine nodded. "Sure. It's fine." She felt cornered and didn't want to appear unreasonable or inhospitable to her daughter. What she really wanted to do, though, was rush over to him, beat on his chest with her fists, and tell him to get out of her house. How dare he work his way back into her life like this? For ten long years she'd tried to put him out of her mind. She'd nearly succeeded. Well, at least she could go several days at a time now without thinking about him. But she'd never been able to ignore the fact that he existed— somewhere. She watched in a daze as the two walked away from her, laughing and talking like old friends.

Sunni poked her head back through the kitchen doorway. "You want a glass of milk, too, Mom?"

"For sure," Catherine answered, glad her daughter had thought to include her. "I'll be right there."

Jonah was already seated at the table when Catherine entered the kitchen. He was watching the girl pull three glasses from the cupboard and fill them with cold milk from the fridge. "You play the piano, Sunni?" He winked at Catherine.

The girl broke a cookie in half and dunked it in her glass, giving it time to absorb the milk before answering. "Yep. I'm taking lessons. Sometimes I don't want to practice, but Mom makes me. She says I'll be glad when I'm older."

Catherine traced the rim of her glass with her finger. She wished he would finish his snack and go.

"She makes you, eh? My mom used to make me practice, too, but I had other things on my mind. Like baseball and football. Are you involved in any sports?"

Sunni's face lit up. "Oh, yes! I love soccer and softball. I'm my team's pitcher. And I like to roller-blade and swim and ski and—"

"Wow, you're a real sportswoman!" Jonah took another cookie, broke off a chunk, and popped it into his mouth. "Your mom never played sports, but she used to come to my games. I played basketball."

"Wow! My mom came to your games? She comes to my games, too." She pulled her cookie out of her glass, took a big soppy bite, then pushed the cookie jar toward their guest. "Want another cookie?"

Jonah nodded then grinned at Catherine. "I kind of figured she did. I imagine she's a pretty good mom." He pulled out a third cookie and dipped it into his milk before taking a hearty bite. "She still makes great chocolate chip cookies! She probably even uses the same recipe."

"Yes, I do. Thank you. I'm glad you like them." She tried to block out the pleasant thoughts of the years she and Jonah had been together, but they came cascading back unbidden. She could see Jonah sitting at the table in her parents' kitchen licking the mixing spoon, stuffing himself on freshly baked cookies. "Well, now that you and my daughter have had your afternoon snack, I'm sure you'll need to get going."

She stood awkwardly to her feet and this time extended her hand toward him. "It's been—nice—to see you again."

"Actually," he said, without making a move to leave as he reached for a fourth cookie, "I need to run by the clinic, but I have an idea. I don't have any plans for tonight. How about letting me take you and Sunni out for dinner? Anywhere you want. We can have pizza, steak, or lobster. Your choice."

"Thank you, but we can't," Catherine answered brusquely.

"Please, Mom." Sunni put on her sad puppy-dog look. "Please say we can go. I don't have homework tonight, and pizza sounds sooo good."

Going to dinner with Jonah was the last thing Catherine wanted to do, but she couldn't come up with a single excuse that would sound valid. "Perhaps another—"

"Tell you what," Jonah broke in. "I'll go to the clinic, run by my parents' house and change clothes, then pick you two up around six-thirty. Does that sound okay, Cat?"

Catherine gave him a cold, hard stare.

"Cat?" Sunni covered her mouth and let out a giggle. "You call my mom Cat? That's kewl."

"It's a silly nickname." Catherine picked up the glasses and put them in the sink. "I've asked Dr. Shelton not to call me that. It's a childish name."

The girl clapped her hands together. "I like that name, Mom. I think it's cute!"

"I'm much too old for cute names. My name is Catherine."

Sunni lifted the cookie jar from the table and returned it to its place on the countertop. "You're a doctor? What kind?"

Jonah laughed. "What kind do you think?"

"Umm. Dentist?"

"Nope. Guess again."

Catherine was upset by his banter with her daughter, but she kept silent. She wanted him out of there, plain and simple. *Now.*

"I know. You're a veter—veter—"

He leaned back and laughed heartily. "Me? A veterinarian? A doggie doctor? Nope! I'm afraid not. They'd probably bite me!"

Sunni's laughter filled the little room. "I give up. What are you?"

He jabbed her arm playfully. "Actually, I'm what the public calls a plastic surgeon. Do you know what that is?"

She giggled again. "Sure, I know what a plastic surgeon is. I'll bet you could—"

Catherine leaped forward, placing herself between her child and their visitor. "We shouldn't keep Dr. Shelton, Sweetie. He told you he has to get to his clinic."

She turned to Jonah. "We appreciate the invitation, but we don't want to take any of your precious time away from your clinic." She glanced at him, then her daughter, and added quickly, "Perhaps some other time when you're not so busy."

"But I'm not—"

She wrapped her arms around her daughter and pulled her close. "Maybe your fiancée can join us. Or doesn't she like pizza?" She hated the sarcasm in her voice, but for some reason she didn't seem able to control it.

He laughed, and the dimple on his cheek danced. "As a matter of fact, she hates pizza. But. . .I love it! And I'll bet you do, too, don't you, Sunni?"

"Almost better'n chocolate chip cookies." She smiled brightly.

Jonah gave the girl a thumb's-up. "Good. Then it's settled. See you at six-thirty."

Speechless and feeling defeated, Catherine watched the door close behind him.

Jonah was back in her life.

three

Jonah folded his lanky body into the red Mercedes convertible and, with a frown, inserted the key in the ignition. It had been quite an afternoon. He'd hoped Catherine would have forgiven him by now. He hadn't expected her to welcome him with open arms, not after what had happened between them, but he certainly hadn't expected the open hostility he'd found. After all, it had been ten years. Much too long for anyone to hold a grudge. "But what man understands women? Certainly not me!" he mumbled, shifting the car into reverse.

After backing the car out of the driveway and onto the street, he turned and headed west. He hated the way she glared at him when she talked about the end of their brief marriage. Even though now that he was older he knew he deserved it.

He braked at the four-way stop sign, looked left and right, then crossed the intersection. Well, she had every right to be mad. He remembered how determined his parents had been that night they'd come to the hotel room and taken him away. They'd made their position very clear, and they'd refused to back down. No marriage before college graduation—period!

At the time he'd wanted to spend the rest of his life with Cat. He'd been so sure his parents would adjust to the idea of their marriage, once they realized they were serious enough to run off to a justice of the peace. But he'd been wrong. Dead wrong. They wouldn't hear of it and had their lawyer get it annulled immediately. He remembered crawling into his bed in his parents' house with mixed emotions. They'd shown up at the motel and literally pulled him out of Catherine's arms. No matter how much he defended himself now, Cat was right about one thing. He had used his parents as an excuse instead of taking responsibility for his own actions. And it had never quit bothering him. For ten long years he'd lived with that guilt. It had haunted him every single day. But the past three months had been the worst. Since he'd confessed his sins, asked God to forgive him, and accepted Christ as his Savior, Catherine had been on his mind every waking moment. He had to make things right with her; that was his mission. But, even more than that, he had to make sure she, too, had a right relationship with God. Especially now that he knew she had the responsibility of raising a daughter.

❧

"Mom, may I wear my new pink shirt tonight?"

Catherine shuddered. Why had she ever agreed to this unwelcome invitation?

"Mom? Did you hear me? I asked—"

"I heard you, Kiddo. Sorry—I had my mind on something else."

Catherine shook her head to clear away the image of the handsome doctor. "Yes, the pink shirt will be fine. You look pretty in pink."

Sunni twisted her long blond hair together at the nape of her slender neck and stared into the mirror. "Should I wear a ponytail?"

"I like your hair in a ponytail. I put your pink scrunchy in the top drawer in your bathroom, if you want it."

Catherine took the brush from Sunni's hand and ran it through her daughter's silky hair as she gazed into the mirror with unseeing eyes. Why hadn't she asked for Jonah's cell phone number? If she had, she could call him right now and put an end to this charade. If only Sunni weren't so excited about going. But why shouldn't the girl be excited? How many times did they get an invitation from a handsome man to have dinner at any place of their choosing?

Sunni pulled away and flopped down on her mother's bed,

pointing her long legs toward the ceiling. "Mom, I like Dr. Shelton. He's nice. How come you didn't marry him instead of Daddy?"

Catherine stared at her daughter. She was so young yet so perceptive. "I–I wanted to, but things—didn't work out."

"He was one of your boyfriends, wasn't he?" She flipped over onto her stomach, her gaze never leaving her mother's reflection in the mirror.

"Sort of. There were complications, Honey."

"Like what?" Sunni's question seemed simple enough, but the answer was anything but simple.

Catherine touched the tip of the brush to her chin. "We were both young, and his parents didn't like me."

Sunni sat up straight. "Didn't like you? Why? Everyone likes you."

"I was from a poor family. His parents were rich. Very rich and influential."

Her daughter crossed her arms defiantly. "Well, being poor shouldn't make any difference, if you love someone. Did you love Dr. Shelton?"

Catherine slowly laid down the brush, picked up the comb, and ran it through her own hair as she searched her heart for an answer. "Yes."

"Did he love you?"

"I thought so." She exchanged the comb for her perfume bottle without thinking about what she was doing, her mind centered on Sunni's question. "I guess I was wrong."

"Then why did he come to see you?"

Catherine sprayed the perfume lightly on her neck. That was one question she couldn't answer. One she'd wondered about herself. Why had Jonah come to see her, when a phone call would have accomplished the same thing? Surely that excuse he'd used about being a Christian now wasn't valid. "I guess he was just being friendly."

At six-thirty the doorbell rang, and there stood Jonah, in a paleblue knit polo shirt and blue jeans. To Catherine it was déjà vu. Dressed casually, he looked more like the Jonah she remembered.

"Well, you two ladies look lovely tonight."

"Hi, Dr. Shelton," Sunni greeted him with a bubbly smile.

"Hello, Jonah." Catherine pulled a wisp of hair over her cheek. Were the long skirt and eyelet top too dressy for pizza? Well, it was too late to change. Besides, what difference did it make? She no longer had a reason to care what this man thought about the way she looked.

"Cat, you look beautiful." Jonah reached out his hand to assist her with her jacket.

Ignoring both his compliment and his offer, she struggled into the garment by herself. She felt as nervous being around him as a first-time jumper on a bungee cord might.

Sunni stooped to tie her tennis shoe. "I'm so hungry for pizza, I'm gonna eat six pieces."

"Sunni!"

He strode over to the girl and wrapped an arm about her slim shoulders. "Me, too. Let's go!"

The Pizza Kingdom was crowded. They had to settle for a small corner table meant for only two chairs instead of three.

"Maybe we shouldn't stay," Catherine suggested as they sat elbow-to-elbow around the tiny table, their knees touching.

"And miss this atmosphere?" Jonah yelled above the blare of the jukebox. "What do you think, Sunni? Stay here or go someplace else?"

"Stay!" The glow from the candles in the red glass containers on the table reflected in the child's eyes. "I like it here. Can we have pepperoni with extra cheese?"

Jonah leaned toward Catherine, nudged her side with his elbow, and winked. "Pepperoni and extra cheese? That's my favorite, too, Sunni. How did you know?" He turned to

Catherine. "Is that okay with you, Mama? As I recall, you always liked pepperoni."

"I. . .guess. If it's what you two want, it's fine with me," she yelled back.

After the waitress brought their order, Jonah reached out and took Catherine's and Sunni's hands in his. "Mind if I pray?"

She gave him a curious look. *Is this for real or an act?* "Aren't you carrying this Christian thing a bit far?"

He smiled at her pleasantly. "You may not believe it, Cat, but Christ is an active part of my life now—in everything I do, even asking Him to bless pizza."

Sunni chuckled. "Some of my friends pray when we eat lunch at school. I think it's kinda neat, but I've never heard a man pray for pizza before."

"Well, you're going to hear it now." Jonah squeezed her hand and closed his eyes. "Thanks, God, for allowing the three of us to have this pizza together tonight. Bless it to our bodies, and please bless our fellowship together. In Jesus' name I pray. Amen."

"Wow," Sunni said, smiling up at Jonah, her eyes big as quarters.

"Have at it!" Jonah used the spatula to lift the largest piece and place it on Sunni's plate.

Sunni started eating with enthusiasm. As Catherine watched them, she couldn't help but remember the pizzas she and Jonah had shared. What wonderful times they'd had. She'd been the envy of all the girls in her class. He was a real catch. Handsome, wealthy, the leading scorer on the school's basketball team and, best of all, nice. They were always together. She'd been sure their love would last a lifetime. She'd never thought of it as puppy love, as their parents had called it. Looking back now, even Jonah must have thought it was puppy love. Otherwise. . .

"Mom!"

Sunni's voice, straining above the music, interrupted Catherine's thoughts. "What?"

"Dr. Shelton asked if we could go to the hockey game with him this weekend. Can we go? Can we? Please, please?"

"No, Sunni." Catherine glared at the man seated beside her. "We have plans for the weekend, remember? We're going to shop for some spring clothes for you, and we need to—"

Her daughter's lower lip turned down in a pout. "Mom! That's not going to take all weekend."

Catherine looked at the doctor again. *Why did you have to do that?* "I'm sure Dr. Shelton has more important things to do. It's very kind of him to—"

"Actually," he broke in, "my weekend is free, and I happen to have tickets for the Saturday night hockey game. I'd like to take you two—that is, if Sunni would like to go."

Sunni's eyes glittered. "Sure, I want to go. I can hardly wait to tell my friends. They'll think it's neat!"

"We'll discuss it later and let Dr. Shelton know tomorrow, Sunni," her mother told her with an exasperated sigh. No sense discussing it now when she was outnumbered, she decided.

"Okay. But I really want to go." The girl seemed to accept her mother's answer as a maybe and delved back into her pizza.

Catherine felt uneasy and out of place sitting beside Jonah in such an intimate setting, their elbows and knees touching in the crowded quarters. But, she had to admit, she was enjoying his company. She was afraid, though, that anyone seeing the three of them snuggled up around that little table eating their pizza would assume they were more than just friends.

One of Sunni's classmates from school and her parents came in and were seated a few tables away. Sunni asked to be excused so she could go over and say hi. Catherine didn't want her to go; she didn't want to be left alone with Jonah. But her daughter insisted, and she finally agreed to let her.

Catherine toyed with the crust of her pizza, struggling to

avoid Jonah's eyes. She looked everywhere but at his face.

"Do you hate me that much, Cat?" he finally asked in a hushed tone, scarcely audible above the noise of the jukebox.

She picked up her crust and took a small bite, still avoiding his eyes. "I—I don't exactly hate you, Jonah."

He cupped her chin with his hand and gently directed her face toward his. "Don't exactly hate me? What's that supposed to mean?" She tried to turn away, but he held fast.

"I really loved you, Jonah. I thought you loved me, too," she whispered softly, half hoping the music would drown out her words.

"I did love you, Cat. But the timing was wrong. I needed to concentrate on school, not a new wife. At least, that's what my parents convinced me I should do. Can't you understand how things were for me then? They were my parents." His words were soft and kind, but they hurt, nonetheless.

"No, I can't understand how things were for you, as you call it. Perhaps if we hadn't—"

His grip relaxed, and his hand fell into his lap. "But we were married at the time."

Catherine took a deep breath and let it out slowly. "Briefly."

He smiled again as he took her hand and squeezed it gently. "I should've been stronger. We might have made it on our own without my parents' help. But I guess we'll never know that, will we?"

"I always thought we could make it," she said, her voice filled with emotion. "I was willing to do my part. I thought love conquered all."

He looked around then lowered his voice. "I'd hoped to remarry you—eventually. Maybe after I finished med school. That's what I wanted to tell you that Christmas when I came looking for you, but you were already gone."

"Marry me again? After you'd dated around to make sure you didn't want to marry some other girl? Or your parents would prefer you'd marry? Give me a break, Jonah. I may not be as educated as you, but I'm smart enough to know it may never have happened. Not if your parents had their way, which they always seemed to." She could feel her anger rising with each word and was sure her cheeks were turning pink.

"I have to admit, Cat, that I've felt lower than an earthworm every time I've thought about you. As I've grown older, I've finally realized the magnitude of what I did to you, and I'm so ashamed. You were the innocent party in all of it. You knew my parents were opposed to our marriage, but you married me in good faith, expecting our marriage to last. Like a coward, ignoring the vows I'd just taken before God, I let them separate us. You deserved so much more. I wish I could make it up to you somehow. Just tell me how, and I'll gladly do it."

Catherine sat with her hands folded in her lap, his knee touching hers, and struggled against the tears that threatened to spill over.

"That's why I showed up at your door today. I had to make sure life had been good to you. I stopped by your parents' house several times during Christmas vacation that December after I went to college. But your mom said you'd moved to Wichita, and she wouldn't give me your address or phone number. I even called the Wichita information operator, but there was no listing for a Catherine Hayley. I wanted to tell you I was sorry for the way things had worked out for us and apologize—tell you I hoped you'd still be there when I graduated from college."

She glared at him. "What do you mean, 'worked out for us'? It sounds as though your life went on the way the three of you planned. Without my being part of it!"

He bent his head. "I just wanted to apologize for—well, you know—what happened between us that night. But, I have to admit, it was the most wonderful thing I'd ever experienced."

"I'm ready to go home now." Sunni arrived at the little table and grabbed her denim jacket from the back of her chair. "You guys ready?"

Her daughter's timing was perfect. Catherine had wanted to shout at Jonah that their only time together, as husband and wife, had been the most wonderful experience of her life, too. She'd thought she'd go mad if she had to sit next to him another minute.

Sunni sat in the front seat of the Mercedes and babbled all the way home about the friend she'd seen at the pizza place and the hockey game Jonah had invited them to. Catherine had managed to be the first one in the convertible and opted for the backseat, preferring to be blown away by the wind than to share the front seat with Jonah. When they reached home, he insisted on walking them to the door, despite her protests.

"Have you made up your mind yet, Mom? Can we go to the hockey game with Dr. Shelton? Please," Sunni pleaded as she bounced backward up the sidewalk in front of them.

Catherine fumbled in her purse for the key to avoid seeing the disappointment in her daughter's eyes. "No, I don't think so. Some other time, maybe."

The girl quit bouncing and stopped dead still in the middle of the walk, blocking their way. "Aw, Mom. You always ruin all my fun. Why can't we go? He wants us to go with him—don't you, Dr. Shelton?"

Jonah looked at Catherine. "I don't think your mother wants to go. Perhaps she doesn't like hockey."

"She does, too! She watches it on TV with me all the time." Sunni grabbed her mother by the hand. "Please, Mother. Say yes. It'll be fun."

Catherine bit her lip. She hated denying her daughter anything that was within her power to grant, as long as it wouldn't harm her. But this?

Jonah finally said, "Why don't I call your mother tomorrow—

after you two have had a chance to talk it over? Okay?" He tugged on the girl's ponytail before turning to her mother. "I've enjoyed our evening. I hope you'll let me take you to the hockey game. You and Sunni."

Before she could tell him to leave and never come back, he turned and was gone.

Once they were in the house and the doors had been secured for the night, Sunni dropped into a chair and kicked off her shoes. "Now look what you've done!" She frowned. "A really nice guy asks us out, and you chase him off. What's the matter with you, Mom?"

Later, in the semidarkness of her bedroom, that question ricocheted in her mind.

What was wrong with her?

Here she was approaching thirty years old and virtually an old maid. She hadn't spent time with a man since. . . She shuddered at the thought. A shaft of moonlight triangled across her bed. She'd nearly forgotten what it was like to be held in the comfort and safety of a loving man's arms, to feel the thrilling touch of his lips against hers. But the touch of Jonah's knee against hers at the pizza place had brought it all crashing back.

She flipped over and stared at the ceiling with unseeing eyes, trying to envision what life would've been like if she and Jonah could have stayed married.

Then she looked at the clock on the nightstand and wondered what he was thinking about after spending the evening with her and her daughter.

She turned her back to the window and pulled the covers over her head, trying to block out the handsome face of the doctor who'd arrived on her doorstep that very afternoon. No, she had to stay away from Jonah. What was over was over! He'd mentioned his fiancée. There was no more possibility in the future for a relationship with Jonah now than ten years ago. When he called, she'd tell him they absolutely could not go to the hockey game, and she'd appreciate it if he didn't contact them again. Yes, that's exactly what she would do.

☙

It was quiet in the Shelton house that night when Jonah entered the foyer. What a day this had been. He was finally able to apologize to Cat, even though she hadn't accepted it. It had been a rather haphazard apology. He hadn't intended to say what he did nor as late in his life. Over the past ten years he'd tried a number of times to get her address or phone number, but she seemed to have vanished. Several of their former classmates had heard she'd married and moved away, but no one knew exactly where she was—or wouldn't tell.

Oh, her parents and her sister probably knew, but he had decided not to ask them. They had been angry at their breaking up and would have offered little cooperation. He had tried, especially in the past three months, to find her. Since he'd become a Christian, Catherine was constantly on his mind and heart. He was glad he'd received a letter from the reunion committee about updating their high school classmates' files. God had answered prayer. It took him only one call, and he had Cat's married name, address, and phone number.

He grasped the handrail and moved quietly up the curved staircase that led toward his old room. *Well, Catherine Hayley-Barton, I'm not giving up that easily. I owe you, and I'm going to do everything in my power to make things up to you, whether you like it or not.*

"Jonah? Is that you?" Horace Shelton was standing on the upper landing in the darkened hallway, dressed in his lounging robe and leather slippers. Jonah had been told he looked very much like him, despite the silver streaks in his father's hair.

"Yes, it is, Dad."

His father flipped the switch on the wall, filling the stairwell with light. "I've been worried about you, Son. I thought you'd be home for dinner. Alexandra has been calling every half hour from New York. She said you were supposed to phone her back, but you never did."

Jonah took the stairs two at a time to the landing. He wondered how much he should tell him about his whereabouts. "I've been visiting an old friend."

"Old friend? Anyone I know?"

He had the feeling his father was prying, although he'd given his parents no reason to suspect he would consider contacting Cat. No one in the Shelton house had brought up her name for years.

"No, probably not." He gave his father's shoulder a loving jab. "Good night, Dad. I've had a big day. I'm going to turn in early."

Jonah tried to sidestep him, but the older man grabbed his son by the shoulders and spun him around. "Don't do anything foolish, Jonah. You and Alexandra have a good life ahead of you. She'll make a fine doctor's wife. Your mother and I like her, and she's the kind of woman we've always wanted in the Shelton family."

Jonah stepped quickly away from his father's grasp. "Since you and Mother were the ones who picked her out, why don't you two marry her? Or, better yet, we could have a marriage ceremony for the four of us, and we could all say, 'I do!' We could live here in this mausoleum and be one big happy family."

"Jonah!" Horace Shelton stared at his son, his only child. "What's gotten into you? I've never seen you this defiant. I think you owe me an apology."

Jonah allowed his frown to soften a bit. This seemed to be his day for apologies. "I'm sorry, Dad. I know you want the best for me, and I appreciate it. Really I do. But I feel as if I'm being pushed into this marriage. You and Mother know Alexandra much better than I do. I'm not at all sure she's the one I want to spend the rest of my life with—that's all."

The older man's face reddened with anger. "Well, now is a fine time to decide that! All of our friends are expecting you two to get married. Your mother and Alexandra have already set the date and are talking to the caterers. I think they've even booked the church! I know they'd planned to shop for Alexandra's wedding dress on this trip to New York."

Jonah's palm came down hard on the railing. "That's exactly what I mean, Dad! I haven't even thought of proposing to Alexandra, and you two have me married to her! Don't you think I should have a say in this?"

The older man seemed surprised. "You haven't proposed?"

"You haven't seen a ring on her finger yet, have you?" His words came out more harshly than he intended, but he was tired of having his life dominated by other people.

His father thrust his hands into the pockets of his monogrammed robe and raised his brows. "No, I guess I assumed you hadn't found the ring you wanted yet."

Jonah shook his head. All his life he'd done what his parents wanted or expected him to do, except for dating Catherine. They'd picked the college he should attend, the fraternity he should pledge, and the cars he should drive. His mother even picked the clothes he should wear. Or at least she thought she did. When he was in high school, he often changed them at a friend's house. Fortunately, when it came to his chosen profession, the three of them agreed. He wanted to be a doctor, and they wanted the same. It had been his lifelong dream to be a physician like his uncle Bert. Uncle Bert had been the one who'd encouraged him to become a plastic surgeon, even though his parents were determined he should specialize in cardiology. But with his uncle's persuasiveness they'd changed their minds and admitted being a plastic surgeon would be as prestigious and every bit as lucrative.

"Dad." He wished he could have gone to bed without this

confrontation. "I'll soon be thirty years old. Although I'm just beginning my career, I'm on my way to becoming a highly respected physician in a very competitive field. And, along with Uncle Bert and his partners, we've opened a second clinic. Don't you think it's about time you and Mother let me start living my own life?"

His father's head dropped. "That's the way you feel, Son—as if we've been pushing you into this marriage?"

"Yes, that's exactly how I feel."

"Your mother and Alexandra are going to be very unhappy if you break things off with her."

Jonah let out an exasperated sigh. "I haven't decided to end my relationship with Alexandra, but I haven't decided to marry her either. So far we've spent very little time together. I don't think I even know the woman. Not really. I'd like to take my time, date her, and maybe some of the other women here in Dallas. If things work out for the two of us, fine. Otherwise, I hope we can part as friends. You know how reluctant I've been to marry, and with good reason."

His father snickered. "You don't know women very well, do you, Son? They don't take kindly to a man breaking up with them."

Jonah rubbed at his forehead. "I know that, Dad. From personal experience! Remember? At your insistence I broke up with the only woman I've ever loved."

"Surely you don't mean Catherine? Wasn't that her name? That girl you dated in high school?"

Jonah let out a long sigh and nodded. "Yes. Catherine. The girl I loved and left when I stupidly allowed you and Mother to make a farce of our short marriage."

His father shrugged and glanced at the grandfather clock in the hallway. "It's past my bedtime. I suggest you forget about that unfortunate teenage incident and phone Alexandra before you retire. She's waiting for your call."

Jonah felt like yelling a rebuttal to his father for that remark—for calling his marriage to Cat an "unfortunate teenage incident"—but he would never do it. He was too much of a gentleman, and he loved his father. Since becoming a Christian, he'd witnessed to his father and mother several times, but they hadn't wanted to listen and took offense at his telling them they were sinners. Someday they would face God, and the thought terrified him. Despite their interference in his life, they were his parents, and he knew no one could witness to them or have concern for their souls as he could. *God, help me to be the witness You would have me to be.*

After retiring to his room, he knelt beside the bed, his head resting on his hands, his eyes shut. *Lord, why didn't I tell Cat the real reason for my visit? I wanted so much to tell her that three short months ago I asked You to come into my life and take control. I promised, with Your help, to make amends for the wrongs I've done in my life. Setting things straight with Cat was number one on my list. I'm afraid I botched things with her, Lord. I didn't even have the nerve to go ahead and fully explain my relationship with You, and how she needs You, too. Please give me another opportunity—and the courage.*

It was nearly eleven before he dialed the phone.

Alexandra answered on the first ring. She was angry with him for not calling her sooner and demanded to know where he'd spent his evening.

He grasped the phone and took a deep breath, wishing he hadn't called and had gone directly to bed instead.

"Alexandra, it's time you and I had a talk."

four

All day Catherine eyed the telephone on her desk. Each time it rang, her hands became clammy. She'd rehearsed her speech over and over, with the firm resolve that she would say no to Jonah Shelton's invitation. No matter how persuasive he might be or how much it upset her daughter.

She sorted business flyers, worked up outlines, downloaded graphics—everything she did in a normal business day—but her mind wasn't on her work. Creating and maintaining Web pages for her corporate clients demanded not only creativity but accuracy, and today she'd been making mistakes. In addition, the hypertext markup language she had to write and enter into her computer was not in the least bit forgiving. A misplaced dash, bracket, or comma, and it threw everything off.

"Why doesn't he call?" she wondered aloud when the clock chimed noon. He said he'd call today, and she wanted to get this over with—to end her association with Jonah Shelton, once and for all.

She scooted her chair away from the computer and headed for the kitchen. Normally she'd get so busy in her office that she'd forget about lunch until it was almost too late to eat. But today was different. After watching the clock all morning, she was hungry. *Funny how I always seem to turn to food when I'm nervous.* She slathered mustard on her ham sandwich and piled her plate high with potato chips.

She hated eating alone. Jonah had said she was much thinner, and she was. Eating alone was probably one of the reasons she'd lost weight and kept it off. That and keeping up with an active child, who never seemed to run out of energy.

She thought about the many joys of being a mother—her daughter's first smiles, seeing her sit up for the first time, her first tooth, watching her first steps, taking her to kindergarten that first day of school, listening to her struggle with words as she learned to read, attending her first piano recital. A tear of pride made its way down her cheek, creating a path for others to follow. She dabbed at her eyes with her sleeve. Too bad Sunni's father hadn't been able to share those wonderful moments.

Despite her eagerness to end things with Jonah, she allowed the phone to ring four times before she quit staring at it and crossed the room to pick it up.

"Sis? Hi, it's me. I drove by your house last night and banged on the door. You weren't home, but your car was there. Are you okay?"

Catherine relaxed her grip on the phone. "Hi, Joy. I'm—fine, I guess."

"You guess? What does that mean? Are you sick? Or is something wrong with Sunni?"

"No, I'm not sick, and Sunni's fine."

"Then what's wrong? Something is. I can sense it, and I can hear it in your voice."

Catherine slid onto the tall kitchen stool in front of the breakfast bar. "Jonah's back." She could hear the gasp on the other end of the line.

"Jonah's back? Have you seen him yet?"

"He came by yesterday. Unannounced. It was a shock to see him at my door."

"Did he apologize? Is that why he came by?" Joy asked, her voice filled with concern.

"I guess you could call it an apology. He took us out for pizza. And get this, Joy. He's moved back to Dallas!"

"You went out for pizza with him?" Joy asked.

"Yes, and he invited us to the hockey game this—"

Her sister broke in. "You're not going, are you? I heard he's engaged."

"No, we're definitely not going. But Sunni wants to go so badly, I'm afraid I'm going to have trouble with her when she finds out I've told him no. Those two really hit it off."

"Oh, Catherine, you don't need this. It's taken you years to get to this point with your life and your business. First you lost Jonah. Then Jimmy. You can't set yourself up to get hurt again. Especially not with Jonah!"

"Don't worry. I'm going to tell him no. He was supposed to call me today, but so far I haven't heard from him. I hope he's realized by now that I don't want him in my life, so he'll leave me alone. It'd be the best thing for everyone."

"Did he mention his fiancée?"

Catherine let out a long sigh. "Barely, but he did say he's semi-engaged. At least, that's what he called it."

Joy snickered. "Semi-engaged? I never heard of that one. What's that supposed to mean?"

"Who knows? It's a new term to me, too. She called him on his cellular phone yesterday while he was here. He said something about her being in New York on a shopping trip with his mother."

"She must have culture, breeding, and money, if old Mrs. Big Bucks is accepting her for her son," Joy said mockingly in a falsetto voice. "She wouldn't settle for anything less. But I guess I don't have to remind you of that, do I?"

"I'm not excusing her, Joy. But now that I'm a parent I better understand Jonah's mother's reasoning. She only wanted the best for her son. In her warped opinion and the opinion of his father, I wasn't the best. It's that simple."

"Well, you're being kinder than I would be under the circumstances." Joy groaned. "Every time I see her picture on the society page, I want to scratch her eyes out for what she did to you."

"If Jonah loved me as he said he did, he would've stood up to his parents. I guess I should realize he never loved me at all. He just wanted—"

"Stop that kind of talk. I was there! I saw the two of you together. I know he loved you."

"Well, he sure had me convinced; otherwise, I—"

"I know, Honey. I know."

❧

It was exactly 3:20 when the red Mercedes convertible pulled up in front of the grade school and parked near the crosswalk. Jonah hadn't been able to get Catherine and Sunni out of his mind all day. He drummed his fingers idly on the steering wheel to the beat of the music playing on the car's gospel radio station. It was a beautiful day, and on impulse he'd lowered the car's top and let the warm sunshine stream in. It felt good to be back in Dallas. He'd missed it. He wondered how long it'd been since Catherine had moved back. It couldn't have been too long ago. Hadn't she said she'd only lived in that house a couple of years? He'd asked about her each time he'd come home for a visit, and no one had seemed to know where she was.

He glanced toward the big glass doors on the front of the grade school, then at his watch. Soon hundreds of kids would come streaming out. He hoped he'd be able to spot Sunni in the crowd. In fact, he hoped he was at the right school.

"Hi. I heard you were back in town."

He spun around to see a beautiful young woman approaching. She looked very much like the one he'd enjoyed pizza with the night before. "Joy? If I hadn't seen Cat with her longer hair, I'd have thought sure you and she were the same person. You two still look amazingly alike."

"Hey, thanks. I'll take that as a compliment. What are you doing here outside the school? You don't have kids going here, do you? Catherine said she thought you were engaged, but she never mentioned anything about kids."

He laughed. "Nope, not me!" The idea of his having children was ludicrous. He'd never really had a wife, except for that one day with Catherine.

She frowned and eyed him suspiciously, leaning one hand against the edge of the windshield. "You're not planning to pick up Sunni, are you? How did you know this was her school? I doubt my sister would have told you."

"Just a good guess. Since this grade school is only a few blocks from her house, I figured I'd take a chance on its being the right one." He shielded his eyes from the bright sun with his hand. He wasn't pleased with the way she'd stated her question. "What if I am here to pick her up?"

Joy's eyes widened. She leaned forward, both hands gripping his door. "I don't think Catherine would approve. Besides, that's my job. I pick Sunni up every afternoon on my way home from work. That way Catherine doesn't have to quit in the middle of one of her clients' projects."

"Her clients' projects?" Suddenly he realized he knew very little about Cat's life. He'd never even asked if she was employed. "What does she do?"

Joy's brows rose. "She didn't tell you? She has her own business—she creates and maintains Websites for a number of major companies. She's so good at it that she has a waiting list of businesses who want her to do their Websites. She works from home and has one of her bedrooms set up as an office. She's doing very well, and working at home makes it possible for her to be there for Sunni."

"I'm happy to hear that, Joy. It sounds like the ideal arrangement."

She stepped back and looked his car over from bumper to bumper, then gave a low whistle. He wondered if she was looking for a way to change the subject. "Guess doctoring pays pretty well, huh?"

He smiled. "I'm doing okay, but I would feel better if your

sister would forgive me for deserting her on our wedding night. She still hates me for it, Joy. I saw her yesterday."

She nodded. "I know. She told me. What did you expect? You and your parents really hurt that girl, Jonah. She was crazy about you."

He looked down. "Being sisters and close friends, I suppose she told you—I—we—"

"Yep, she did."

"I've never forgiven myself for leaving her that way," he murmured.

"Then why do you expect her to forgive you—when you can't even forgive yourself? What you did was pretty cowardly."

For the first time Jonah realized he was asking Cat to do something he hadn't been able to do himself. Why should he expect her to forgive him? Perhaps under the circumstances he was asking too much of her. God had forgiven him, but why should she?

The outside buzzer sounded loudly on the school building. At once the glass doors flew open, and the yard was flooded with students wearing book bags and racing off in all directions.

"There she is!" Joy shouted above the noise and waved her arms over her head. "Sunni, over here! Here I am!"

The young girl flashed a big smile when she spotted her aunt and the red convertible and hurried over, leaving her friends behind.

"Hi, Aunt Joy. Hi, Dr. Shelton. What are you doing here?"

"I'd like to take you home if it's all right with your aunt Joy."

Sunni smiled and clapped her hands together, then turned to her aunt. "Oh, please, Aunt Joy. May I ride home with Dr. Shelton?"

Joy looked from one to the other as she shook her head. "I don't think your mother would—"

Jonah cut in. He was determined to see Cat again, and

taking Sunni home might provide the excuse he needed. "You can trust me, Joy. Honest. I'd never let anything happen to Cat's child. Please? Let me take her home. It's only a few blocks. I'll take her straight there, I promise."

"Please, Aunt Joy?"

Joy looked from Jonah to her niece and back again and sighed. "Tell you what. Let me phone my sister and ask her permission. If she says it's okay, it's fine with me."

Jonah grimaced. *Uh-oh. That probably means a big no!*

She dialed Catherine's number on her cell phone then turned her back to him. Jonah wished he could hear their conversation, but with Sunni chattering away about some boy in her class he caught only a word or two from Joy's side.

Finally she hit the off button and stepped closer to him so her niece wouldn't hear. "She's not too keen on the idea, but rather than having to explain to Sunni why she's not certain she can trust you—"

"She can trust me, Joy. I've grown up. I'm not that silly kid I once was. I—"

Joy put her hand up. "You didn't let me finish, Jonah. As I said, she wasn't too keen on the idea until I told her I'd follow you in my car."

He brightened. "Does that mean—?"

"Yes, but remember—I'll be right on your rear bumper. She said you must bring Sunni straight home, Jonah. Do you hear me? No side trips. That girl is everything to Catherine."

"Straight home," Jonah agreed, crossing his heart. He smiled and nodded to Sunni, who tossed her book bag into the backseat and eagerly climbed in beside him. "I promise, Joy. You may not believe it, but I am different now, and I take my responsibilities seriously."

Joy waggled her finger. "You'd better take them seriously, or we'll both be in trouble."

The young girl giggled, then waved to her classmates as

the convertible pulled away from the curb with her aunt close behind.

"Have a good day at school?" Jonah asked, glancing at his passenger with a smile.

"Uh-huh—really good. I made a hundred on a math test, and I was chosen to sing in the all-school chorus."

"Wow! That is a good day. You must be very good at math. Math was one of my favorite subjects, but I rarely made a hundred on a test." He looked in the rearview mirror and saw Joy following in her car.

Sunni waved to someone in a passing car. "But the best part of the day was my friends seeing me drive off with you."

He smiled at her. "Why? Because we're in a convertible with the top down on a beautiful day?"

She shook her head and giggled again. "No, because most of my friends have a father or stepfather who picks them up sometimes. I've never had a father to pick me up. I wonder if they think you're going to be my father—since you're picking me up today."

five

Startled by her words, he slowed the car down and looked over at her. "Your father? Me? I don't think your mother would want to hear you say that! How long has it been since your father died?"

She turned around and waved to her aunt, her face beaming. "Oh, Mom says it was before I was born. I never saw him, and he never saw me," she said matter-of-factly. "So I've never really had a father. Just a mother. Do you have a father and mother, Dr. Shelton?"

He flipped the directional signal, wheeled around the corner, and headed the car down the street. "Yes. Both."

She smiled. "You're lucky. I wish I did. It'd be nice to have a father to play catch with. My softball coach says I need someone to help me practice my pitching, but my mom's not much good at catching." She giggled again. "Or throwing— but she tries."

He decided to push for a little more information, though he told himself it didn't matter. "Doesn't she have a boyfriend who could help you practice?"

"My mother have a boyfriend?" Her eyes widened. "Are you kidding? She's never had a boyfriend, not since my daddy died."

He pulled the car onto Cat's driveway and turned off the key. "Why not? She's beautiful and intelligent. It seems to me lots of men would be after her."

Sunni shook her head. "Nope. She doesn't want a boyfriend."

Jonah muttered an almost inaudible, "Oh."

The girl shrugged. "Maybe it's because you broke her

heart when she was in high school, and she didn't want it to happen again."

Jonah was silent. He didn't know how to answer, or even if he should. He took a deep breath, then motioned for Sunni to remain seated while he jumped out of the car and hurried to the other side to open her door. He reached for Sunni's book bag. "Let me take this for you. I want to say hi to your mom and find out about the hockey game."

Joy, who'd parked her car behind his in the driveway, walked up quickly to join them.

He wrapped an arm about Sunni's shoulder, and they all headed for the front porch.

Catherine met them at the door, a frown on her face. "Sunni, how many times have I told you to ride home with your aunt Joy? I don't want this happening again!"

Joy held up her hands. "I told them, Sis. That's the reason I called you."

Jonah stepped between them, hoping to ease the situation he'd caused. "I promised Joy I'd bring Sunni straight home, and that's exactly what I did, even though I wish we could have stopped for ice cream."

He watched Catherine's face. She was even more beautiful now than she had been as a teenager and possessed a natural beauty he'd rarely seen. And, whether he liked it or not, he found himself attracted to her, as long-buried feelings began to surface.

"Ice cream?" Sunni asked. "You wanted to stop for ice cream? Yummy!"

He smiled down at the girl, then glanced at her mother. "Uh-huh. We didn't dare stop on the way home since I promised your aunt I'd bring you here by the shortest route. But perhaps we could convince your mother to leave her computer long enough to run to the ice cream shop in the mall. Maybe we could get a double-dip chocolate ice cream cone or a banana split. Your aunt Joy can come, too."

Joy shook her head and began to back away. "Count me out. I have things to do." She turned toward Jonah. "And don't put me in the middle again, Jonah. I don't like being there. Just be sure you don't. . ." She glanced at Sunni, who was staring at her with big eyes, taking in her every word. "You know what I mean."

He nodded as she hurried toward her car, glad she hadn't said any more in front of the child.

Catherine started to say something but stopped. He noticed that the frown on her face had faded slightly. As soon as Joy's car was out of sight, he said brightly, "It's a pretty day. I put the top down on the convertible."

Her expression softened a bit more. If she said yes, he knew it wouldn't be because he'd asked her; she would do it for her daughter rather than disappoint her.

"Please, Mom?"

Catherine wrapped an arm about her daughter's slim shoulders and pulled her close. "As long as we're not gone too long. I'm working on a tight deadline." She gave Jonah a look. He could tell he was in big trouble for even mentioning ice cream.

"Thanks, Mom!" The girl turned and raced into the yard ahead of them toward the red convertible. "Yippee! Ice cream!"

Jonah handed the book bag to Catherine and waited until she'd placed it inside the door before shutting it behind her. Then, putting his hand lightly in the small of her back, he started to guide her to the car.

She drew in a quick breath, then let him lead her down the sidewalk without even looking back or frowning at him.

Sunni insisted her mother sit in the front seat. Catherine avoided his gaze, but Jonah could tell from the slight smile on her face that she was enjoying the ride. Sunni talked almost constantly from the backseat, leaving Catherine and Jonah free not to speak. He had spent little time around children and found himself enjoying the girl's bubbly presence, as well as that of her lovely mother.

"Are you going to pray for our banana splits, Dr. Shelton?" Sunni asked once they'd given their orders to the waitress.

"Would you like to do it?" he asked in return.

Sunni giggled then looked at her mother with a questioning gaze. "I don't know how."

Catherine glanced back at her daughter. She was silent for a moment. Finally she said, "God quit answering my prayers a number of years ago."

"Maybe you just quit asking," Jonah inserted gently.

"You do it, Dr. Shelton."

He grinned at Sunni, then bowed his head and thanked God for their banana splits.

Sunni chattered on about school, clothes, and sports while they all enjoyed their cold treats around a small wrought-iron table at the ice cream parlor. Suddenly she asked, "Mom, are we going to the hockey game with Dr. Shelton?"

"No, Honey, we're not."

Cat's quick response surprised Jonah. He had thought she was warming up to him since she'd allowed him to take them for ice cream, but apparently not. "Oh, come on, Cat. It's only a hockey game."

"I'm afraid of those flying pucks I've seen on TV." She kept her gaze focused on the banana she was slicing with her spoon.

Sunni's smile faded. "Mom! That's silly."

Jonah was sure Cat was using that as an excuse. "No problem. I have box seats on the second row behind the protective glass. No pucks are going to hit us there. We'll be perfectly safe. Say yes, Cat—please." He wished she wouldn't be so stubborn. Surely spending an evening at a hockey game would do no harm. He knew Sunni would enjoy it. And it would give him another opportunity to ask for Cat's forgiveness.

"Well. . ."

Jonah could sense that she was weakening, but rather than pressure her any more and perhaps bungle it, he decided to let her daughter persuade her.

"Say yes, Mom—please."

"I still haven't decided. I'm not sure this is a good idea. Let me think about it a bit more. All I'm saying now is maybe."

Sunni said nothing more.

Jonah turned to her. "I'd better take you two back home now so your mom can work."

The ride home went all too fast for Jonah. As far as he was concerned, Saturday night and the hockey game couldn't come soon enough, providing Cat said yes.

&

"Mom, why don't you like Dr. Shelton anymore?" Sunni asked when her mother tucked her in for the night. "I think he's nice."

Catherine smoothed the covers, then sat down on the edge of the bed. Perhaps it was time to explain what few things she could about the relationship between her and this man who'd so suddenly dropped into their lives from out of nowhere. She stroked her daughter's cheek. She was so beautiful. To look at her now, with her big blue eyes and blond hair, Catherine couldn't imagine life without her. She thought nothing could ever compare to the joys of motherhood.

"Honey, I don't dislike him. Not really." She paused, wondering just how much she should say. "I—I think you're old enough now that I can talk to you about him. About us."

Sunni gave her a look of exasperation. "Mom, I'm nearly ten!"

Catherine gazed into Sunni's innocent face. In eight short years her daughter would be the same age she was when she and Jonah had married. Before long she'd have to talk to her about the birds and bees—or whatever they called it these days.

Her daughter tugged on her sleeve. "Mom, I'm waiting. Are you going to tell me or not?"

Catherine stiffened. This was going to be even harder than she'd imagined; but she knew she had to do it with the way Sunni was getting so attached to Jonah.

"Well, when I was in junior high, I met Jonah."

"Junior high? Really? I'll be in junior high in three more years."

Catherine smiled, kissed the tip of her finger, and transferred the kiss to her daughter's nose. "I know you will. Anyway, he was the best-looking boy in my class. We became friends almost immediately. I was terrible in math, and he used to help me with my homework. He was always a whiz at math."

"Like me? All my friends say I'm a whiz at math."

"Yes, Sweetie, like you."

She continued. "During our first year in high school, Jonah invited me to his birthday party. He invited Joy, too. We hadn't realized how rich the Shelton family was until we went to their house for that party. They lived in a mansion. I wish you could have seen their furniture."

"It was pretty?"

Catherine nodded, remembering how she and Joy had walked through the house with their mouths open. They'd never been in such a grand house before. "Oh, yes, Honey. It was the prettiest house I'd ever seen. They had a huge swimming pool in their backyard. That's where the party was held. There were balloons everywhere and tons of ice cream and the fanciest cake you could imagine. All of Jonah's friends and relatives were there. Most of them your aunt Joy and I had never met."

"Did they play games?"

She transferred another kiss to her daughter's forehead. "No, not games. But they had hired a couple of magicians, who put on a wonderful show. Your aunt and I had never been to such a fancy party."

Sunni's eyes brightened. "Did you and Aunt Joy wear fancy dresses?"

Catherine stared at the hole that was forming in the knee of her jeans. "No, we didn't own fancy dresses. Actually, we were both a little embarrassed when we showed up in our school dresses. The other girls were in their Sunday best." She donned a melancholy smile. "We didn't have Sunday best dresses! We wore the same dresses to school that we wore for dress-up."

"I'm sure you looked as pretty as those other girls," Sunni said, smiling up at her mother.

"We didn't feel pretty. We felt poor, especially when Jonah's parents talked down to us."

Sunni's eyes widened. "Talked down to you? What does that mean?"

"That means they weren't very nice to us. When we showed up, they asked us to leave. I don't think they even knew Jonah had invited us. I'll never forget feeling so out of place."

"Was Dr. Shelton nice to you? Did he tell his parents he'd invited you?"

Catherine nodded dreamily. "Oh, yes He was very nice. He told his parents and tried to make us feel welcome, but he had other guests at the party besides us. His parents were still rude and made us feel like intruders. Anyway, despite that, in time I became his girlfriend."

She chuckled. "He told everyone we were going steady. But the funny part of it was, we never went anywhere! He was too young to drive, and my parents said I was too young to date, so most of our times together were spent on my parents' porch swing."

"That's neat," Sunni said. "Kind of old-fashioned. I like it—it's sweet."

"Like in the olden days—way back when?" Catherine laughed. "Before electricity was invented?"

"Something like that," Sunni said, her blue eyes twinkling. "At least he didn't drive a covered wagon!"

"Well, I'm only telling you this so you'll know why I don't want to be friends with him."

Sunni rose up on one elbow. "Was he mean to you, too?"

Catherine gazed off in space, remembering. "Oh, no. Jonah was a real gentleman. We had such a good time together. When he was old enough to drive, his parents bought him a car. Not a covered wagon!" she said, pinching her daughter's arm lightly. "His parents didn't know we were dating—he'd kept it a secret from them—but we still managed to spend every possible minute together. By the end of our senior year we were talking about getting married."

"Really?" Sunni's eyes widened. "Why didn't you marry him? I like him. He's nice. Was he as nice as my daddy?"

Catherine's heart tightened. "Almost. I thought we were going to get married. He'd even given me an engagement ring."

"Do you still have it?"

"Yes, I keep it in a little box in my desk." She'd never told anyone she still had that ring—not even Joy.

"Why haven't you showed it to me?"

Catherine searched for an answer and finally said, "I will if you want me to. Anyway, I knew Jonah was planning to go to college. I thought we would get married and I'd go with him. Oh, not to attend college. I knew I could never afford that. But I thought I could work, keep the house clean, and make sure he had clean clothes to wear and good food on the table."

"So what happened?"

Catherine chose her words carefully. Sunni need never know about their brief wedding. It would serve no purpose. "His parents said we were much too young to be so serious. They made Dr. Shelton break things off with me."

"They did? That wasn't very nice. Not if you loved each other! I read a library book like that once, where the girl was poor and the boy was rich."

Catherine took a deep breath. It was hard to explain things

without revealing the whole truth—that they had expressed their love fully once, on their wedding night, and then his parents had taken him away. "I'm sure they thought they were doing the right thing, but I was crushed. So was Jonah. He left for college that next morning."

"What did you do?"

"Well, two weeks later I moved to Wichita. With Jonah gone I had no reason to stay in Dallas. As poor as my parents were, I decided it was time I moved out of the house and made it on my own."

Tears formed in her daughter's eyes. "Oh, Mother, that is such a sad story. It's just like a movie."

Catherine blinked back her own tears. "But this story didn't have a happy ending as the movies do, Honey. I never heard from Jonah again. Not once in all these years."

"So you met my daddy and married him?"

"Yes."

"And had me?"

"Oh, yes! You'll never know how happy and excited I was when the doctor told me I was going to have a baby. Then you were born, and I took one look at your precious little face, and I knew I'd love you forever. I loved you so much that I rarely let anyone else hold you, not even your aunt Joy! I know that was selfish of me, but I wanted you with me, in my arms, every second of every day. I loved everything about you. I even loved changing your smelly diapers!"

Sunni held her nose. "Yuk!"

"And now that you're nearly ten, I realize you won't be with me forever, and it makes me sad. All too soon you'll be old enough to date, and I'll have to share you and your time with someone else."

Sunni wrinkled up her nose. "I don't think I want any boyfriends. All the boys I know are silly."

Catherine laughed. "You think that now. But I guarantee

you that someday, when you're older, a special boy will come along and sweep you off your feet, and—"

"Like Dr. Shelton did you?"

She cringed. "Sort of, I guess."

"Do you still love Dr. Shelton?"

"Of course not!" Catherine swallowed. Something stirred inside her, and she knew her daughter's question might be too close to the truth. She had loved Jimmy very much, but seeing Jonah again had rekindled old feelings—feelings she had tried so hard to bury long ago.

"Do you think he still loves you?"

"No!" Catherine tucked the covers beneath her daughter's chin and stood quickly to her feet. "He didn't love me then either. At least not enough to defy his parents and stay with me. They did everything they could to break us up. You can't believe how angry they were when they discovered we were"—Catherine paused—"secretly dating."

Sunni's serious gaze met hers. "When I have a boyfriend you won't do that to me, will you, Mom?"

For a moment Catherine considered the question from a mother's point of view. "I hate to admit it, Sweetie, but if I thought the boy was wrong for you I'd probably do exactly what they did. But I would be kinder about it." She moved to the door and turned out the light. "Sleep tight, Baby. I love you."

"I love you, too, Mama."

Before Catherine went to bed, she walked over to her desk, pulled out the little white box from the back of the drawer, and tugged on its blue satin ribbon. In the box was a lovely but small diamond engagement ring—the ring Jonah had given her the Christmas of their senior year. Next to it was a narrow gold wedding band with two little entwined hearts engraved into it. She slipped both rings on the third finger of her left hand. A tear trailed down her cheek. *Oh, Jonah, I loved you so much.*

She brushed away the tear, placed the rings back in the box, and returned it to its place in her desk. Then she made her way into the bathroom and took off her makeup. She brushed her hair into a ponytail, a style she reserved for sleeping, then slipped into her gown and crawled into bed with a book she'd been intending to read. She hoped its words would help her put Jonah Shelton out of her mind. She knew sleep would not come easily, no matter how hard she tried. The story line was good, but she had a hard time keeping her mind focused on the words. Jonah's face kept popping up before her. Unlike Joy, who had never wanted to get married, Catherine had wanted nothing more out of life than to be the perfect wife and mother. Jimmy had been a model husband and the best friend she'd ever had. She'd loved him. She'd honestly loved him. They'd had a good marriage, and if he'd lived he would have been a wonderful father to Sunni.

What was that noise?

She sat straight up in bed and pulled the covers tightly about her shoulders. The fear of someone breaking into her house was always with her, and the nightly news reports on television only fueled her fears. That was the reason she rarely watched them.

The noise sounded again.

Her heart pounding, she slipped into her robe, pulled the little container of mace from between the mattress and box spring, and moved cautiously into the hallway.

When it sounded the third time, she realized the repetitive sound was coming from the living room. Someone was tapping lightly on the front door!

She relaxed a little. Joy had mentioned something about a meeting and that she might stop by on her way home. She'd probably seen her bedroom light as she was driving past and decided to stop for a sisterly chat, as she did quite often.

Catherine flipped on the porch light and peered through the peephole in the door.

It wasn't her sister who was standing there.

It was Jonah.

She cracked the door several inches. Then, before she could ask him what he was doing on her porch at that time of night, he pulled open the storm door and stepped inside.

That was when he saw it.

six

Catherine grabbed the scrunchy holding back her hair, but it was too late.

Jonah gasped. "What happened to you?" His hand reached out to her cheek. "Where did you get that scar?"

She tried to pull away, but he grasped her wrist and held her fast.

"Cat! Answer me!"

She finally jerked loose and tugged the scrunchy off, letting her hair fall free.

He gently pushed the hair away from her cheek, revealing the jagged scar she'd tried so desperately to hide. Slowly he traced the raised edge with his fingertip. "Oh, Cat, whatever caused that awful scar? That's why you're always tugging at your hair on that side. I can't believe I never noticed it."

She wanted to push his hand away, to tell him it was none of his business, but he was so gentle, so like the Jonah she'd fallen in love with, that she couldn't. No matter how much she wanted to resist his concerned attention, she found herself letting him wrap his arms around her and draw her close. The feelings of hurt and hatred that had haunted her all these years seemed to be melting away. She found herself under his spell once again. She had to resist. Ten years of hurt couldn't be cancelled out by one casual evening and a few words of regret.

She held her breath. There was something so safe in Jonah's touch, yet dangerous.

"Cat," he pleaded softly. His chin grazed her forehead, and he continued to hold her close to him. "Tell me what happened to you."

When she didn't answer, he touched her chin with his finger-tip and lifted her face to his. "Please. Tell me. I need to know."

"I—I'd rather not. It was a long time ago." She tried to back away, but he stopped her.

"Cat, please. I'm concerned about you. I know what scars like that can do to someone."

She knew he was telling the truth. No doubt surgeons like him, who routinely did reconstructive surgery, saw injuries like hers every day. Maybe if she told him, he would leave.

She struggled to keep her composure and willed her heart to be still. "When we were moving, I was carrying a box of dishes down a flight of stairs, and I tripped. Some of the dishes broke, and I fell on top of them. That's it. Not much of a story, I'm afraid."

His fingers moved back to the scar. "You got that scar from falling on broken dishes?"

"Yes, broken dishes." She hoped her story sounded credible and tried to pull away, but he held on to her, preventing her escape. Fooling a doctor, a plastic surgeon, might not be as easy as she'd hoped.

"Turn toward the light. I want to have a better look."

She didn't want to turn toward the light, to let him examine the scar she'd worked so hard to conceal, but she felt that she must. She turned her head slightly.

Jonah slipped his fingers beneath her chin, tilted her head more, then lifted a thick lock of the straight brown hair and tucked it behind her ear. "Oh, Cat. That scar runs from nearly your chin, back up over your ear, and into your hairline. You're telling me broken dishes did that?"

She nodded. He had to believe her. She hadn't let anyone get close to that awful scar, except her family, her daughter, and Jimmy, and the doctors who had sewn it up when it happened.

He separated the hair on her scalp and followed the scar as it naturally parted her hair. "You must've had quite a bit of bleeding with a nasty cut like this."

She nodded again.

❧

Jonah's finger traced the scar again. "I find it hard to believe a long, continuous cut like this could have come from broken dishes." She was lying about the scar. There was no doubt about it. He'd seen too many injuries, patched up too many people, to believe a serious injury like that could be caused by a fall on broken dishes. But why would she lie about it? It didn't make sense. He felt compelled to learn the truth.

"Did you see a plastic surgeon?"

"No! I couldn't afford one." She tried again to pull away from his grasp.

She was uneasy. He could see that. For some reason she apparently didn't want to go into the details of her accident. But why? What would keep her from telling him the truth? "Did you break any bones in your fall?"

"No, but you needn't be concerned. It happened a long time ago. I rarely even think about it."

He tilted her chin upward again. "You were lucky you didn't break your back—or fracture your skull. Was it the whole flight of stairs?"

"Yes. No. I can't remember. It all happened so fast."

More lies. "Were you alone at the time? I hope not. With a cut like that, you could have bled to death."

"Ah—a neighbor was there—well, she came later—"

Why wouldn't she look at him? Was she making up her answers as she went along? If he'd had a serious accident like that, he would remember every second in great detail. It may not be any of his business, but he was determined to learn the truth. "Was it before Sunni was born?"

"Yes."

"Then you were already married?"

She nodded but still avoided his gaze. "Yes, but Jimmy wasn't home. He was at work."

After moving the lock of hair from behind her ear and allowing it to fall back over her cheek, he took her hands in his and looked directly into her eyes. "I could fix this, you know," he said with great concern. It was a deep scar, but he'd seen his Uncle Bert repair others much worse than hers, and he knew they could do it.

"No. I—I couldn't afford it. I'm saving every spare penny for Sunni's college."

She stepped back, but he kept holding her hand, then led her to the sofa and motioned for her to sit down. *Is this how You're working it out, Lord, so I can repay Cat for the heartache and grief I've caused her?*

"Look, Cat. I hate to brag, but I'm getting to be a pretty good plastic surgeon. I've helped my Uncle Bert perform a number of operations on people with problems like yours. That guy is a master."

She lowered her head and examined each of her fingers one by one. "As I said—I can't afford—"

Jonah dropped down beside her, put his arm around her, and pulled her close to his side. "Don't worry about the cost! That's not an issue. Our surgical team will do it for free, and we can get the hospital to use your operation as a teaching session. It won't cost you a dime."

She lifted her chin high in the air and stared at him through misty eyes. "I'm not a charity case, Jonah. I pay my own way. I always have."

"You won't be a charity case. You'll be doing both me and the hospital a favor. Let me do this for you. Please. What good is being a doctor if you can't help someone you—?"

"I—don't think so, Jonah."

He could name at least a dozen patients who would jump at the chance he was offering her. He could think of no reason she should refuse, unless she was afraid of the surgery.

"You're beautiful, Cat—even with your scar. But our surgical team can fix it so you can wear your hair any way you want to."

"I'm not self-conscious."

"You're not? Then why are you constantly tugging at your hair? I've seen you do it, Cat. Many times. I'm sure others have noticed it, too." He selected his words carefully; the last thing he wanted to do was offend her. "Is it that you're afraid of the surgery?"

She let out a long sigh. "A—a little, I guess."

"That's all that's stopping you? A little fear, when you have so much to gain?"

"No, that's not all," she confessed, lifting her gaze to meet his, her jaw jutted forward. "As I said, I'm not a charity case. I never have been. Not even—"

Jonah waited, but she didn't finish her sentence. Well, that approach didn't work. He tried to think of another one. Then it hit him. A way to get her to say yes.

"Would you do it for your daughter?" He was confident he'd found her tender spot. He knew she'd do anything for her child.

God, please help her say yes! I want to do this for her. Maybe in some small way it will make up for the hurt I've caused her. You've blessed me so much by allowing me to become a doctor. But none of it means anything if I can't use it for Your glory. Perhaps, through this surgery, I can reach Catherine's heart and show her how much You love her and how committed I am to making things right between us. Maybe through this I can gain her forgiveness as You've forgiven me. I want her to know I've committed my life to You, and I'm willing to do whatever You would have me do. No matter what it is or how much it demands of me.

She lifted misty eyes to his. "Well, maybe if she wanted me to. Oh, I don't know. I've lived with it so long. It's been a constant reminder of that—" She stopped midsentence and gulped.

"Reminder? A reminder of what?"

"Of—of my fall," she said quickly, before the words had scarcely left his mouth. "A reminder of my fall."

He leaned his head against hers and nuzzled his chin in her hair. It was good to be holding her again after all this time. He felt like a schoolboy stealing precious moments with the girl he loved as he planted soft kisses in her hair. When she didn't pull away, he carefully parted her hair and trailed gentle kisses along the scar, following it from its beginning high in her hairline, over her ear, down her jawline.

She emitted a small sigh as she ever so slightly lifted her cheek to accommodate him.

When he reached her chin, he didn't stop and moved right to her lips. She was still attractive, even more so as a grown woman than she had been as a teenager, and he hadn't been able to resist her then.

Suddenly he felt as if they were being transported back ten years, to when they'd been high school sweethearts, as she accepted his kisses. They were no longer doctor and computer expert, but boyfriend and girlfriend of yesteryear. Old longings took over. His heart responded in ways he hadn't experienced with the other women he'd dated. He wondered if he'd made the worst mistake of his life when he hadn't stayed married to Catherine Hayley.

"Let me fix that scar, Cat," he murmured between kisses. "Please. It's the least I can do for you." *Please, God, work this out!*

❧

If ever Catherine felt out of control, it was the moment Jonah pulled her into his arms. When he kissed her, it was as if she'd stepped onto a magic carpet reeling backward through time. There was something so sweet, so compelling, about his words. There was an aura of masculinity about him. Perhaps it was because he was nearly a decade older now. Perhaps it was because the love she'd once had for him was reawakening.

"Cat? Did you hear me?" He said the words softly as his

kisses traveled along the scar and followed its path back into her hairline. "I'll fix it so it's barely visible. Wouldn't you like that?"

Reality struck.

What was she doing?

She struggled to free herself from his grasp, raising her hands to repel his advances. "What do you think you're doing?"

He seemed stunned by her sudden reversal. "I don't know, Cat. I was looking at your scar, thinking how I could fix it for you, and you seemed so small and helpless. I wanted to take care of you." He held out his hand. "Oh, what am I saying? All of that is true, but I also wanted to kiss you."

Catherine refused his outstretched hand. "Have you forgotten? You're engaged!" She turned away from him; yet all she wanted to do was run into his arms. "Or is it semi-engaged?"

He took a step forward. "Look—Alexandra isn't wearing a ring. I haven't given her one!" he nearly shouted.

"Shh!" Catherine motioned toward Sunni's room.

He lowered his voice to a whisper. "I haven't even decided if I ever want to marry her, and I've told her as much."

She brushed her hands over her eyes and hurried across the room to the door. "I think you'd better go, Jonah. It's late, and I'm tired. I'm sure you are, too."

She could feel the tension in the room, and she was miserable. The nerve of the man, kissing her like that!

His shoulders drooped, and he headed for the door.

She suddenly realized she didn't know why he'd appeared at her door this late. "Why did you come by tonight, Jonah? I wasn't expecting you."

"I'm not sure this is the right time to talk about it."

"Whatever it is, now is probably as good a time as any."

"I came to talk to you about Sunni." He stood in the doorway, pulled in a deep breath, then let it out slowly. "I think that little girl needs a man in her life. I'd like to be that man, if you'd let me."

She blinked hard. *Jonah Shelton in my daughter's life? Never!* "What makes you think she needs a man in her life?"

"She told me so."

She couldn't believe Sunni would ever tell him such nonsense.

"She did, Cat. Honest. She said her coach told her she needed to find someone to catch balls so she can practice her pitching. I could do that."

"I do that already!"

A slight smile curled his lips. "I know. She said you weren't very good at it."

Her frown eased. She had to smile in spite of herself. "I try."

He stepped toward her cautiously. "I know. But I could do better."

She didn't want to argue with him. She simply wanted him to go. "Look, Jonah. I appreciate your offer. But what my daughter doesn't need is to get attached to someone and have that person move on with his life when he gets tired of playing the Good Samaritan. I know you mean well, but we can't accept your offer or your charity."

"Dr. Shelton?" Sunni came into the room, rubbing her eyes and carrying her teddy bear in her arms. "How come you're here?"

He swept the child up in his arms and touched a finger to her nose. "I–I came by to see if you and your mother have decided to come to the hockey game with me."

"Did she say yes?" Sunni asked, then gave a big yawn.

"I think she'd better tell you, Kiddo." He nodded toward her mother.

Catherine hated being put in the middle. If she said no, her daughter would be upset with her. If she said yes, she'd be upset with herself. She lost either way. "I don't—"

"Mom! Pleeease! I've already told my friends Dr. Shelton invited us."

"I'm sure Dr. Shelton can find someone else to take to the

hockey game. Maybe one of his doctor friends."

"But I want to take you and Sunni."

Catherine looked from one anxious face to the other. "Sunni, I'm sure Dr. Shelton has other things going on in his life. It was very kind of him to ask, but we really shouldn't monopolize so much of his time."

"Let me worry about my time. Say yes, Cat, please. Then, if you still want me out of your life, I'll go."

She hesitated. She'd had to deny Sunni so many things in her life. If Jimmy were alive, he would be taking their daughter to all sorts of sporting events, playing catch with her in the backyard, maybe even coaching her softball team. Was it right to refuse her this opportunity to see a live hockey game?

"All right, young lady," she said. She wanted to make sure Sunni understood she wasn't giving in because the child was begging. "We'll go, but just this one time. That's it."

"Yippee!" Sunni yelled. She threw both arms around Jonah's neck and gave him a bear hug, before calling out to her mother, "Thanks, Mom. I love you!"

"I love you, too. Now go on to bed. Tomorrow's a school day."

Sunni planted a big kiss on Jonah's cheek as he lowered her feet to the floor. "Good night, Dr. Shelton." She ran to her mother and repeated the bear hug. "Good night, Mom."

They watched the girl go before resuming their conversation.

Jonah touched his cheek where Sunni had kissed him. "Hey, I could get used to this. Being kissed by two beautiful women in the same evening."

Catherine frowned and turned her face away from him. "I didn't kiss you. You kissed me."

"But you enjoyed it as much as I did. Come on—admit it."

"I got carried away—that's all. For old times' sake."

She couldn't help but laugh. The whole situation was so ridiculous.

He slipped an arm about her waist and walked beside her

to the door. "You certainly have a beautiful daughter. She looks a lot like you."

She smiled. Compliments about her daughter were always welcome.

His grip tightened. "Her father must have been a handsome guy. She didn't get those long legs and that blond hair from you."

She winced. "He was handsome. In my eyes one of the most handsome men I've ever met. Inside and out." Her tone was melancholy. "He loved us both dearly—even though Sunni was yet to be born. We were his life."

"Wow, Cat! You really know how to cut a man's ego down to size. What about me? You used to tell me I was the most handsome man you'd ever met. Have I changed that much?"

Her only response was a smile. His boyish grin and his kidding stirred up deeply buried emotions she wanted to forget.

He glanced at his watch. "I'd better go and let you get some sleep. Pick you up Saturday about five?"

She looked at him. "I thought it was an evening game. What time does it start?"

He grinned sheepishly. "Seven-thirty. I thought maybe you'd let me take the two of you to dinner first, to celebrate."

"Celebrate? Celebrate what?"

He bent and planted a quick kiss on her lips then hurried toward the door. "That you let me kiss you without slapping me."

She pushed open the storm door and gave him a gentle shove. "We'll be ready by five. See you Saturday."

Catherine closed the door and leaned against it, listening as he started his car and backed it out of her driveway. She wondered how she could love and hate someone at the same time.

❧

The streets were nearly deserted as Jonah drove home, but he didn't notice. His mind was still back at the Barton house. He'd half-expected Catherine to slam the door in his face, but she hadn't, and he thanked God for it. He didn't know what would have happened if he hadn't prayed about it before going to see her. While their conversation had been strained, at least they'd been able to talk, and that was a step in the right direction. If only he could make things right between them. At times during the past ten years his guilt had nearly caused him to give up the idea of becoming a doctor. How could he treat patients who placed their lives in his hands when he'd failed the one person who had loved him the most? The one who had trusted him with her life?

He smiled as he thought of her daughter. What a delight that child was, and how much joy she must bring to Catherine. And Catherine! Wow! She was even more beautiful than he remembered.

He'd enjoyed being around both of the Barton women, and he was going to see them again. He chuckled aloud. "Yes, this has been quite an evening. It went much better than I imagined. The last thing I expected to do when I rang that doorbell was to kiss Catherine Hayley-Barton."

The answering machine in his bedroom was blinking when he entered. He listened to a message from Alexandra telling him to call her when he got home; she didn't care how late it was. She wanted to talk to him.

He took a shower, crawled into his pajamas, and went to the kitchen for a glass of juice before sitting down on the edge of the bed and dialing the number.

She answered on the first ring.

"What's so important that I had to call you tonight?" He leaned back against the headboard and took a sip of juice.

"I just needed to hear your voice, Sugar. Your mother and I have been having a delightful time shopping in New York. You can't believe the gorgeous things I've found for my trousseau. I bought a marvelous sapphire blue suit, with matching shoes, of course. A designer dress to die for, a swimsuit and pareo covered with sequins, and—"

"Trousseau? You're shopping for your trousseau?" Jonah shut his eyes and clenched his fist in frustration. "Isn't that a little premature, Alexandra? We aren't even engaged. Or are you planning on marrying someone else?"

There was a brief silence on the other end. "But we are going to be married, aren't we, Sugar? I mean, we've been talking about for a long time. I—I just assumed we—"

He hated it when she called him "Sugar." "*You've* been talking about it! You know I've never agreed to marriage, Alexandra. We've discussed this time and time again."

"But your parents—"

"I am not ready for marriage. With Uncle Bert's Denver clinic getting on its feet and the opening of the new clinic, getting married is the last thing I want to do right now."

"But, Sugar, all our friends think we're getting married. Your mother is helping me plan the wedding!"

He drew in a deep breath. He didn't want to hurt her, but he knew he didn't love her. "Alexandra, I'm sorry, but—"

She interrupted with a teary voice. "Oh, Sweetheart, let's talk about this when I get home. You're just tired from making that ol' move from Denver. You'll feel differently when you can hold me in your arms. I'm coming home tomorrow, and we'll talk then, okay?"

What could he say? If he intended to straighten this situation out with her, at least he could do it face-to-face, not over the telephone. "Tell Mother hello for me. I'll see you both tomorrow. Have a safe trip."

He lay awake for hours. Life was sure complicated sometimes. He'd spent the last ten years working toward the career he now had. By now he should be ready to share his success with a mate. Alexandra was a fine woman. Beautiful, sophisticated, a member of Dallas's social set. Everything a man could want. The kind of woman his parents would be proud to introduce as their daughter-in-law.

But she wasn't right for him. He didn't love her.

❧

"How did the pizza thing go?" Joy asked with a grin the next morning as she strolled into her sister's office.

Catherine typed a few more lines, hit the save button on her computer, and leaned back in her chair with a sideways smile. "Fine, I guess. Sunni had fun."

Joy stared at her. "Why do I get the feeling there's more to your story than a simple 'fine'?" She walked over to the coffee-maker sitting on the counter next to the scanner and poured herself a cup.

Catherine locked her hands behind her head. "As usual, Joy, you're right. There is more. Yesterday afternoon I saw Dr. Jonah Shelton, and last night I saw the old Jonah Shelton I once loved and pledged to spend the rest of my life with."

Her sister leaned toward her. "Oh, Sis, be careful. Don't open yourself up for more hurt."

"I'm not, Joy. But we're both grown-ups now. Perhaps it's time for me to forgive him. He thinks I'm carrying a grudge. He may be right. Maybe what I've been calling hurt feelings is nothing more than a grudge."

"You didn't tell him anything, did you? About your accident?"

Catherine shook her head.

"I really think you should. He needs to know."

Catherine stared at the ceiling and answered with a sigh. "I thought about telling him. He gave me the perfect opportunity."

"Are you going to do it?"

She thought for a minute before answering. "No. I don't think so. It would serve no purpose, except to make him feel responsible."

Joy balanced the cup on her knee precariously. "So—instead you told him to get lost?"

"I tried."

"Tried?"

"He's taking Sunni and me to the hockey game tomorrow night."

Joy grabbed the cup before it tumbled off her knee, then sat up straight in her chair and stared at her sister. "He's what? I thought you were going to send him away. You told me he was engaged!"

"Semi-engaged. I was, but he—"

"He what, Sis? Do you want to be hurt again?"

"He saw my scar, Joy. He wants to fix my face."

Joy's face brightened. "Oh, Catherine, that would be wonderful. He owes it to you. You've been so self-conscious about that awful scar."

"I have not!" she exclaimed. "That's what he said, too—that I must be self-conscious because I keep tugging at my hair. Neither of you knows what you're talking about!"

"Did you tell him you couldn't afford it and that's why you haven't had it done?"

"Sort of." Catherine shrugged. "According to him, it won't cost me a penny. I'd be part of some kind of hospital teaching program."

Joy put her hand on Catherine's arm and smiled at her sister. "You're going to do it, aren't you? Have the surgery?"

Catherine hesitated. "I–I don't know. Maybe not. I haven't decided. I certainly don't want to be in his debt. A clean break would be best for everyone."

"But what an opportunity, Sis! I'd take him up on it. Besides he owes you something for messing up your life."

"That's not all, Joy."

"Oh, no—more? What? I can tell by your expression that it's a biggie. What happened? Did you two have a knock-down-drag-out fight?"

"Worse."

"Worse? What could be worse than that?"

"He kissed me," Catherine said with a shy grin.

Joy's mouth opened. "Jonah kissed you? You're kidding."

"No, I'm not kidding."

"Whew!" Joy leaned back in her chair and, with a smile, cupped her hands to her ears. "Details. I want details."

Catherine could feel her face grow warm. "Well, after I tucked Sunni in, I went to bed. I was going to read for awhile, and then I heard someone knocking on the front door. I thought it was you, but I checked through the peephole anyway. It was Jonah. I'd put my hair up in a ponytail, as I always do at night. He rushed in and saw my scar before I had time to pull the scrunchy off my hair."

"Oh, Catherine. I'm so sorry. I know how you've tried to keep that thing covered up. What did he say?"

"He could tell I was upset about his seeing it, and he put his arms around me as if to comfort me. Then he asked about it."

"You let him put his arms around you? I find that hard to believe, the way you've felt about him these past ten years!"

"At first I was angry. Very angry. I never thought I'd be able to let him get near me again, but he was so tender. So caring. In some ways Jonah's different now. He's stronger. Independent. I hate to admit it, and I'd never tell anyone except you, but it felt good to be in his arms again."

"But I thought you said—"

How could she make her sister understand her feelings when she didn't understand them herself? "I know. I said he was engaged. I asked him about that. He claims the whole engagement thing was her idea—that he'd never even asked her to marry him."

Joy frowned. "More—tell me more."

Catherine could feel the warmth spreading up her neck again. "Oh, Joy, please don't make fun of me. You're the only one I can talk to about this."

Joy reached over and patted Catherine's hand. "I'm not making fun of you, Sis. I just don't want you to get hurt again. Go on—tell me what happened."

Catherine looked down. "I–I couldn't believe how natural it felt to be in his arms, Joy. First thing I knew, he was nuzzling my hair with his chin."

"He was?"

"Yes." Catherine glanced up. She felt a little foolish telling her sister what had happened. "Then—then he began kissing my scar—"

Joy's eyes widened. "Your scar? Really?"

"Yes." She pointed to the area with her finger. "From where it begins in my hair, over my ear, and along my jawline. Before I knew what was happening, I felt his lips touch mine."

"What? He kissed you on the lips? I can't believe you let him!"

Catherine shuddered with pleasure as she relived the moment. "Oh, Joy, the feeling was exquisite. Promise you won't make fun of me. I know I should be careful, and I'm trying to be—I really am. I'm only telling you this because I know I can trust you."

Her sister nodded, her eyes still wide with surprise. "You know you can. What happened next?"

"Nothing!" Catherine laughed. "Sunni came in! Our voices woke her up."

"Did she see him kissing you?"

Catherine shook her head. "No, I'm sure she didn't."

"And?"

"And he left! But not before I agreed to let him take us to dinner and the hockey game on Saturday night."

Joy shifted in her chair then leaned forward, looking directly at Catherine. "I thought you were going to tell him to get lost. I guess that kiss changed your mind."

"I was going to tell him, but he and Sunni have taken a real liking to one another. I didn't know how to let her down so she'd understand without explaining about our wedding.

She still doesn't know we were married, and I want to keep it that way."

Joy stood and moved behind her sister then started massaging her shoulders. "You could have a real problem brewing, you know. You're playing kissy-face with a semi-engaged man. Boy, would the elder Sheltons go into shock if they knew about that!"

"It was a simple, sympathetic kiss, Joy. Nothing more."

"Yeah," her sister said, her brow raised. "He probably kisses all his patients like that."

Catherine bent over and lowered her head. Her sister's kneading felt good. She hadn't realized how tight her neck and shoulder muscles had become. Spending eight hours a day at the computer didn't help either.

"He claims the marriage thing is her idea. Hers and his parents'. He says he's not ready for marriage. Who knows if he's telling the truth?"

Joy pressed her thumbs into her sister's neck muscles. "You think he'd lie to you?"

Catherine turned to face her sister. "Why not? I'm lying to him, aren't I?"

seven

"Mom, are my jeans dry yet?"

Catherine looked up from her work with a frown. "You're going to wear jeans tonight? I thought maybe you'd wear that cute—"

"To a hockey game? I'd look like a dork." Sunni giggled as she plopped down in the chair opposite her mother's desk.

"But," her mother reminded her, "we are going out to eat first. Remember? You wouldn't want to embarrass Dr. Shelton, would you? When he was nice enough to invite you? Knowing Jonah, he'll probably take us to some expensive restaurant."

The smile disappeared from the girl's face, and a grimace took its place. "Won't we look silly going to a hockey game all dressed up?"

Catherine reached across her desk and patted her daughter's hand. "At least wear your new jeans. Not those old faded things with the knees out. Maybe with a white tee and that cute jacket your aunt Joy bought for you."

"Okay," Sunni agreed. "What are you going to wear?"

Catherine pushed back in her chair and gazed off into space as she remembered the many times she'd dressed for a date with Jonah when they were in high school. What happy times those had been. Many of the dresses and jeans had been hand-me-downs from their two older cousins, but she and Joy had loved them as much as if they'd been new. A budget for new clothing in the Hayley house had been almost nonexistent during their growing-up years. Any new clothes she had she bought with the money she earned from doing odd jobs at the neighborhood beauty shop after school. She swept up hair, mixed the shampoo concentrates and filled the bottles, dusted, ran errands, and did anything else the owner needed. Her sister had worked behind the counter at a bakery for money to buy her new clothing. The two of them used to share everything. They had to make things go twice as far.

"Mom, I asked you what you were going to wear tonight."

Catherine's mind snapped back to the present. "I—I'm not sure. What do you think I should wear?"

"Those black stretch jeans! You look kewl in those. And that shirt—"

"Sunni! I can't wear those; they wouldn't be at all appropriate. I was thinking of my navy blue pantsuit and the white—"

The girl stuck out her tongue and wrinkled her nose. "Yuk! You'll look like a ticket seller! Don't wear that!"

"A ticket seller?"

Sunni grinned. "Yeah, you know. Like at an airport. That's the way those people behind the counters dress; only they wear that little pin with the wings."

Catherine crossed her arms and propped her feet up on her desk. "Okay, Smarty. How about that long rose-colored knit sweater and my rose and navy skirt? Would that suit you, Miss Fashion Expert?"

The young girl jumped to her feet and planted a kiss on her mother's cheek. "Yes, I like that skirt. So will Dr. Shelton."

Catherine watched Sunni skip from her office, her child's last words still ringing in her head: *So will Dr. Shelton.* Being honest with herself and putting her ridiculous dreams aside, she realized she had to end the relationship between her daughter and Jonah before the two got any closer. To let it go on any longer would only mean disappointment in Sunni's life.

That had to be avoided.

❧

The country club was crowded when they arrived. Jonah had

made a reservation, so they were ushered immediately to a small round table by the huge window overlooking the golf course.

"Wow! This place is kewl!" Sunni opened her eyes wide and scanned the elegant dining room with its crystal chandeliers and heavily embossed tapestries.

Jonah smiled. "The food here is quite good. I think you'll enjoy it."

"Do they have hamburgers? That's what I want—and fries."

"Sure, Kiddo. They probably have anything you want. But before you decide why don't you look at the menu? They have a lot of other things you might like to try." Jonah opened the beautifully hand-lettered menu on the table in front of Sunni and pointed to an item. "Do you like lobster? They have great lobster here."

She wrinkled her nose. "Lobster? Yuk! I'd rather have a hamburger."

Catherine shook her head and gave Sunni a slight frown. "I wish you wouldn't use that word so often, Sunni." She lowered her voice and added, "Especially here."

"Hey, I think some things on the menu are yuk, too," Jonah said and winked at Catherine.

"Really, Dr. Shelton? Like what?"

"Escargot. Oysters. Octopus."

"Yuk." The girl made a face. "Oops. Excuse me."

Her mother smiled. "You're excused. Now you'd better decide what you want. Our waiter is looking this way. I think he's ready to take our order."

Jonah snapped his menu shut. "I know what I'm having, and Sunni has made up her mind. How about you, Cat?"

She paused then closed her menu and placed it on the table. "I'll have what you're having, Jonah."

He signaled the waiter and, as soon as the man had his pen poised over his pad, told him, "Three jumbo hamburgers, medium well-done, on sesame seed buns, cheese, with fries, of course, and three chocolate milk shakes. Large ones." He turned toward his two companions. "Anything else, ladies?"

Both Catherine and Sunni giggled and shook their heads.

"That's it," he said to the waiter with a smile. "And don't forget the catsup, mustard, and mayo."

He smiled to himself as he watched the two seated with him at the table. Catherine had been pretty when she was a teenager, but she was a beauty now. He wondered why she'd never remarried after her husband died. With a face and a figure like that, she—

"Jonah?"

He straightened in his chair, his face warm. She'd caught him daydreaming. "What?"

"I asked if you came here often; then I realized what a foolish question that was. Of course you do. I remember your talking about coming here with your parents."

He reached over and took her hand in his. "I always wanted to bring you here when we were dating."

She pulled back, and he knew he'd hit a tender spot.

"But you couldn't, could you? Your parents would never have allowed it."

"No," he admitted. "I couldn't. But I wanted to, Cat. I was always proud to be seen with you."

She lowered her head. "But only in places where you were sure your parents wouldn't see us."

"Yes, I'm afraid you're right, and I'm not very proud of myself when I think back on it now. I should've stood up to them and made them see how important you were to me."

He stole a glance at Sunni and hoped their conversation wasn't upsetting her. But she was caught up in watching three ladies attempt to eat their lobster with finesse and not succeeding.

Catherine changed the subject then and asked about the clinic, and soon the waiter arrived with their food.

"Oh, that looks good!" Sunni squared her plate in front of her, grabbed a fry, and stuck it in her mouth.

Her mother let out a gasp. "Sunni, use your fork!"

Jonah could see Catherine's reprimand had upset the girl. He could remember many times when his mother had corrected him in that very dining room for his lack of proper etiquette and how bad he'd felt.

"Eat fries with a fork, Cat? That's what fingers are for." With that, he picked up two long, golden fries and popped them into his mouth.

Sunni covered her face with her hands to muffle a giggle.

Catherine grinned and shook her head, then glanced at the nearby tables to see if anyone was watching.

Jonah folded his hands and audibly cleared his throat. "Ah—if you don't mind—"

Catherine and her daughter immediately turned their attention his way. "I—I'd like to pray before we dig in."

Sunni's gaze flitted to her mother then back to Jonah.

Catherine nodded.

Jonah bowed his head and said a simple prayer, ending with, "In Your name, amen." When he finished, he tacked on a silent, *Thank You, Lord, for letting this happen.*

He looked up and smiled at each of his guests, then pointed across the table. "Pass the catsup, Sunni. These things are much better dipped in catsup." He reached toward the girl, who giggled and placed the catsup bottle in his hand.

"You like onions on your burger, Sunni?"

She shook her head, scrunching up her face. "Onions? No!"

"Okay, then I won't eat my onions tonight. I only eat onions if everyone at the table eats them, too." He lifted two onion slices off the sesame seed bun and placed them on his plate, then turned to Catherine.

"You're not planning to eat your onions, are you, Cat?" He was hoping to steal another kiss when the evening was over and didn't want any excuses in his way.

With a grin and a shake of her head, she lifted her onion slices with her fork and set them on the edge of her plate.

Sunni grinned and did the same thing.

"How about mustard on your burger, Sunni? Or are you a catsup girl?" He held up the two containers.

The girl smiled and took them both, adding, "And mayo, too, please."

"Ah, my kind of woman," Jonah assured her as he lifted the burger to his mouth and took a hearty bite. "Umm, good. Try yours, Cat."

When the waiter brought their milk shakes, Jonah was the first to sample his.

Sunni watched then burst into laughter.

Catherine laughed, too.

"What?"

Sunni giggled. "You have milk shake—"

"Jonah!"

The three at the table stopped laughing and turned to stare at the attractive, dark-haired woman standing beside them. She had her hands on her hips and was frowning.

"You have something on your face, Jonah," she said coolly, glaring at him.

He jumped to his feet, grabbed his napkin, and wiped it across his mouth. "Alexandra! What are you doing here? I thought you were going to a banquet or something tonight."

She sent piercing looks at Catherine and Sunni, then turned to Jonah. "I thought you were going to the hockey game with an old friend from school."

Jonah looked at his guests then back at Alexandra, who was still glaring at him. "I am going to the game with an old friend from school."

Catherine started to rise, but Jonah placed a firm hand on her shoulder. He felt as if he were on stage, as if everyone in the place were watching them and listening. He did not like being put on the spot.

"Oh?" Alexandra returned as she crossed her arms and stared at him. "Perhaps you'd care to explain."

Suddenly he remembered he was his own man. This wasn't his mother chastising him. This was his self-declared fiancée. He wasn't about to let her embarrass him or his guests by putting on a scene. He took her arm and leaned toward her.

"Look, Alexandra. Catherine and Sunni are my guests, and, if you must know, Catherine and I did go to high school together. Now you can behave like a lady, and I'll introduce you." He stepped closer to the startled woman and in a hushed voice continued. "Or you can turn around and leave us alone. Your current behavior is not acceptable at this table. Am I making myself clear?"

She jerked her arm free after giving Catherine another piercing look and ran from the dining room. By then the other guests in the restaurant had turned to watch.

"Sorry about that little scene, but let's not allow it to spoil our evening." Jonah could feel the heat in his face, but he smiled at Catherine and her daughter, sat down, and lifted his milk shake. "Ladies, I propose a toast. To us and to a wonderful evening together."

He watched Catherine hesitantly raise her glass. She was so lovely, even with the look of vexation on her face. He knew she was uncomfortable. He felt awkward, too, but he refused to let their evening be ruined.

"Sunni?"

The girl raised her glass. "I've never done this before."

"Well, young lady, I'd say it's about time. To us! The three of us!"

The three glasses clanged at the center of the table.

"Now," he declared, picking up his burger again, "let's eat."

Catherine nibbled on her burger in silence. She found it difficult to get the angry woman out of her mind. So that was the
illustrious Alexandra. She had expected someone more—well,
she didn't know exactly what she expected, but Alexandra was
not at all the poised and in-control woman she'd thought she
would be. This woman was angry and obviously didn't care
who knew it. What a scene she had caused. Catherine had to
respect Jonah for taking care of the situation in such a quick
and capable manner.

She sipped her milk shake and watched Jonah and Sunni
over the rim of her glass. Jonah was putting another dab of
catsup on her daughter's plate. She smiled as he reached
across the table to dip his fries in the red mound. Sunni giggled and tried to shield her plate. They were having such fun
together that she almost felt left out.

"Want some catsup, Cat?"

She turned and looked at him, half aware of what he'd asked.

"Naw, she doesn't like catsup on her fries," Sunni inter-
jected, passing another one through the thick sauce. "She
only likes salt on them."

Jonah offered her the saltshaker. Catherine shook it gingerly
over her plate. She watched them banter back and forth over
the catsup and the fries, and an unwelcome sadness gripped
her heart. This was the first time Sunni had been around a
man for any length of time, other than her grandfather and
her uncles, and she was obviously enjoying every minute of it.

"I need to powder my nose, Jonah. Which way is the
ladies' room?"

He pointed the way, and she turned to her daughter. "Why
don't you come with me, Sunni?"

The girl shook her head. "No, I don't need to go."

Jonah grinned. "She'll be okay here with me. I have a big
stick hidden under the table and will make her mind."

Sunni burst out laughing and nearly sprayed her food across the white tablecloth.

"I won't be gone long. If she misbehaves, you have my permission to whack her with that stick."

As she walked away she heard Sunni giggle again. She hated to leave them alone at the table, but she was glad her daughter was having fun and that her evening hadn't been ruined by the unexpected appearance of Jonah's girlfriend.

Catherine thought the ladies' room was empty. At least, no one was standing in front of the fancy pedestal lavatories. She glanced at the long row of beveled mirrors and headed toward one of the oak-trimmed stalls. Just then a cubicle door opened, and a rather distraught Alexandra stepped out. She frowned when she saw her boyfriend's old school chum.

Catherine forced a smile and tried to step out of the other woman's way, but Alexandra put out her arm to block her. "Who are you—one of Jonah's new goody-goody, religious friends? That man hasn't been the same since he hooked up with that bunch of Holy Rollers and started attending that ridiculous church."

"Religious friends?" Her question made no sense to Catherine. What was she implying?

"That's all he seems to think about these days—that God stuff and he and his uncle Bert's precious clinic!"

Catherine gave her another faint smile. "As Jonah said, I'm an old friend from high school." She tried to keep her voice steady, but the woman's unexpected appearance and her strange words had unnerved her.

The elegantly dressed socialite sized her up from head to toe. "You mean one of his old girlfriends, don't you? I think Jonah's mother may have told me about you. Aren't you the girl who trapped him into marriage before he went off to college?"

Catherine took a deep breath as she fought to remain silent. She didn't want to argue with anyone in the ladies' room. In some ways she felt sorry for the agitated woman. Apparently she cared a great deal for Jonah to cause a scene in the country club, especially in front of people who were no doubt her peers.

"Well, are you?"

"I'm sorry if our presence here tonight upset you, Alexandra." Catherine offered what she hoped would be seen as a friendly smile. "Alexandra is your name, isn't it?"

The woman's face reddened. "So he told you about me, did he? Did he tell you we're engaged to be married this spring?"

That's not the way I heard it. Catherine tried to figure out a way to escape.

"I don't take kindly to women who try to steal other women's men, Miss—"

"Barton. Catherine Barton."

Alexandra threw back her head and let out a boisterous laugh. "You are Catherine! Oh, this is too funny. I'd expected someone who—well, you know—was—"

"Was what?" Catherine could feel the thick hostility in the air.

Alexandra stared at her. "Gorgeous. Sexy. Vampy. I can't believe Jonah Shelton would want to spend his valuable time with someone so—so plain. I mean—you're—you're nothing! Surely you weren't like this when you two dated in high school, were you? Just look at you!"

Okay, lady. Enough is enough. Catherine took a deep breath and held it. She had to get out of there. She quickly stepped away from the woman, put her hand on the ornate brass handle, and pulled open the narrow door. "Look—I'm going into this stall, and when I come out I hope you'll be gone. Jonah Shelton has no interest in me, other than as a friend. Yes, we dated in high school, but that was a long time ago. Now, if you'll excuse me, I'd like to get on with my business so I can return to my daughter and our host."

"Wait! I'm not—"

Catherine slipped into the stall, then called back over her shoulder, "No more. This conversation is over."

To her relief she heard the outside door slam.

Alexandra was gone.

ᴥ

Jonah enjoyed being with Sunni. He wasn't used to spending time around children.

He checked his watch. They needed to be on their way or they'd be late for the face-off at the hockey game—not that it really mattered to him. He liked hockey, but he preferred Catherine and Sunni's company more; inviting them to the hockey game had merely given him an excuse.

"She always takes a long time in the ladies' room, Dr. Shelton," Sunni said, giggling.

"Oh? Don't most women?" He was getting a little concerned. She'd been gone longer than he'd expected. Could she be sick? Had her stomach been upset by the burger and fries? Maybe he should ask one of the waitresses to check on her.

"I can go find her if you want me to."

"No, we'll give her a few more minutes."

He scanned the end of the dining room. Perhaps she'd met a friend, and they were visiting, and the time had gotten away from her. Silly idea. He doubted if her friends would be at the country club. Hadn't she said she'd never been there before?

"There she is." Sunni pointed to her mother.

Jonah rose as she neared their table. "Are you okay? We were worried." She seemed upset about something. He could see it in her eyes.

"I don't want to discuss it now. I'll tell you later," she said in a half whisper, her face flushed and somber. "Could we go now?"

"What happened?" He stepped to her side. "Aren't you feeling well?"

"Your fiancée happened—that's what! She cornered me in the rest room," she whispered, her voice trembling. "I'll tell you about it later. I don't want Sunni to hear."

Jonah motioned to Sunni, then placed his hand in the small of Catherine's back and led them across the spacious dining room.

As promised, their seats at the hockey game were in the second row behind the protective glass, and they made it in time for the face-off, by a mere two minutes.

"Have you ever seen a professional hockey game, Sunni?" Jonah asked over the blare of the arena's organ. "It's pretty exciting."

"No, Dr. Shelton. This is my first." Sunni's gaze flitted back and forth across the ice as the players shot the puck.

"How about you, Cat?"

She smiled. "Mine, too."

Jonah provided them with a running discourse on the game of hockey. Sunni listened closely.

"Three minutes and he can go back on the ice? But his team has to play with only four players until then? Is that right, Dr. Shelton?" She watched a bloody man plop down on the bench in the penalty box.

"Right, Sunni. Hey, you're a smart kid."

Catherine listened as the two talked about icing the puck, crossing the blue line, offsides, facing off, and dozens of other calls. She loved to watch her daughter's eyes light up. She watched her daughter's eyes light up when the team she and Jonah had decided to root for scored points. Perhaps Jonah was right. Perhaps Sunni did need a man in her life. But there was no way she could let Jonah Shelton be that man.

"I'm thirsty," Jonah said, climbing into his car after the game. "How about a root beer? I know a place, a little drive-in, where they serve great root beer in frosty cold mugs. Anybody besides me want one?"

"I do," Sunni chirped from the backseat and raised her hand.

Catherine looked at him, her eyes wide. "Jonah, we had

cold drinks at the hockey game."

"Aw, come on, Cat. Be a sport. The night's still young."

She checked the clock on the dashboard. "It's ten forty-five!"

"What's the answer, Mama?" He grinned, his hands gripping the steering wheel. "An ice-cold frosty root beer or home? It's up to you."

She pursed her lips and raised her brow. "Well, okay. But, Jonah, this has to be the end of—" She paused, not sure how to finish the sentence.

"Of us?" His hand reached to cover hers.

"Yes. Of us."

⁂

The drive-in was busy with Saturday night traffic, and they had to park in the end slot, but Jonah didn't mind. If the service was slow, it would give him more time with his two dates. He loved watching the interaction between mother and daughter. They seemed more like good friends, the way they shared their thoughts and laughed together. But Cat was the mother hen he'd always heard about but thought of only as a joke. The mother whose purpose in life was to make sure her child was happy and cared for and, above all, loved. She was nothing like his own mother, who had always put herself and her own wishes first. Cat was soft and feminine, but Jonah knew that if anyone tried to harm Sunni she would turn into a wildcat. Something he'd heard his pastor say popped into his mind. It was in the Book of Matthew, about chicks being gathered together under the hen's wings. He thought of Cat. He was sure she would do that if she felt her child was in danger, even if it meant losing her own life.

After their order came, they sat there sipping their root beers loudly and laughing and talking. Jonah couldn't remember the last time he'd had such plain honest fun. Sunni was interested in sports, and Cat was all woman. He loved to watch the way her eyes sparkled when she laughed and the way she cocked her head when she listened to Sunni's stories about school. Soon the mugs were empty, and he had no choice but to take the two of them home.

After they stepped out of the car, he slipped his right arm around Catherine's waist and his left arm around Sunni's shoulders and walked the girls to the door. He hoped Catherine would invite him in.

"Thanks, Dr. Shelton. I really had fun." Sunni reached up and hugged him about the neck.

"You're welcome, Sunni. I'm glad you're such a sports fan. I'm sure most girls your age would rather go to a movie or—"

He stopped. "By the way, Sunni, how old are you? You've never told me." He had wanted to ask ever since he first met her.

"I'll be ten in a couple of weeks."

eight

Sunni bounced around the room excitedly, a bundle of energy even at that late hour. "May I stay up and watch a video? I'm not sleepy."

"A video?" Her mother shook her head and wagged a finger in her direction. "Absolutely not! It's bedtime for you, young lady."

"Aw, please. I never get to stay up late like my friends do. Their parents let—"

Jonah tapped his finger on the tip of the girl's nose and smiled into her brooding face. "Sunni, you'd better go on to bed now. Your mother and I have some things to talk over."

The child smiled at him. "Okay, I guess I am pretty tired. Thanks for taking me to the hockey game, Dr. Shelton. I had a great time." She stood on her tiptoes and planted a kiss on his cheek, then turned and kissed her mother. "Good night, Mom." She skipped down the hall to her room and closed the door behind her.

Jonah turned to Catherine, a sudden fire in his eyes. "All right, Lady. You have some explaining to do, and you'd better do it quietly. I'm not sure you'll want to take a chance on your daughter overhearing us."

Catherine frowned. Was he upset because she'd mentioned the conversation she'd had with Alexandra in the ladies' room? She didn't like the tone of his voice. It wasn't her fault the woman had sought her out.

He slipped a firm arm about her waist and ushered her to the sofa. When they were seated, he pulled off his jacket and tossed it onto a chair. Somewhere in the distance a dog barked, breaking the awkward silence between them.

"Well?" Jonah's harsh voice cut into her as keenly as a well-sharpened knife. "I think you have something to tell me."

She wished she'd never mentioned Alexandra. "You needn't be so grouchy. I told you I'd fill you in later about Alexandra."

"Alexandra? I'm not talking about her! I'm talking about your daughter!"

Her brows furrowed. "What does Sunni have to do with it?"

"Don't play games with me, Cat. Sunni said she is going to be ten in a couple of weeks. I don't have my calculator handy, but the way I add things up she would have been conceived sometime around the end of August. About the time of our wedding. Am I right, Cat?"

She could feel his hot breath on her cheek as he leaned toward her. She couldn't see his face, but she could tell from the sound of his voice how upset he was. "She was born prematurely, Jonah," she said. "Many babies are born prematurely."

"Oh, give me a break, Cat. How many months early can a baby be born and still live?"

The sarcasm in his voice frightened her.

He moved closer and took her chin in his hand, turning her face toward him. Even in the dim light of the small lamp on the table, she could see his determination.

"She's mine, isn't she, Cat?"

She stared at him, unable to believe what he was saying. She'd never given him any indication that Sunni was anyone's child but Jimmy's.

"Cat?"

"Of course she's not your child, Jonah," she mumbled. "Jimmy was her father. I've told you that already."

"Oh? She's not my child? Then how do you explain her age? She's going to be ten in a couple of weeks! Do you think I'm an idiot? You never even dated anyone but me, and babies don't just happen. I don't believe your story about

Jimmy. I think you married him to give that girl a name."

For a moment she sat paralyzed by his words; then anger took over. "She is Jimmy's daughter!" she hollered. She jumped to her feet and faced him, momentarily forgetting about her daughter in her bedroom down the hall.

He stiffened, glanced down the hall, then responded in a low, controlled voice. "You're trying to tell me Jimmy was her real father? And you expect me to believe it?"

"Yes."

"I don't remember anyone named Jim Barton! Where did you meet him?"

"At—ah—work."

"You met him at the beauty shop? You never mentioned him to me!"

The doubt she heard in his voice upset her. "He was the owner's son. Older than we were. You wouldn't have known him."

His hand cupped her chin again, and he lifted her face toward his. "Are you telling me you were seeing him when you and I were dating?"

"I knew him, but I'd never dated him. Not until after that night, though he'd asked me many times."

She wanted to cry out and tell him to leave. He had no right to treat her this way.

"You're lying, Cat. You never were very good at lying. I think I deserve to know the truth."

She clamped her fingers over his wrist and pulled his hand from her face, then snapped, "It's the truth, Jonah. When you dumped me, I turned to Jimmy. He was a fine man and good to me. He treated me like a lady. He proposed. I didn't love him at the time, but I knew the two of us could be happy together, so I accepted."

He backed away slightly. "That's the truth? Jim Barton is really her father?"

"Yes," she stated firmly, her heart pounding hard enough to make her chest hurt. "I can show you his name on the birth certificate."

"Birth certificate? That doesn't mean anything. They put any name you give them on those things."

"Then I don't know how else to convince you. You'll have to take my word for it."

He stood and stared at her.

"At first I felt almost guilty for marrying him, as if I were using him, but he never saw it that way." She smiled as she remembered the kind face and gentle ways of the man who'd given her first place in his life. "Over time I learned to love him, Jonah. He was easy to love. And he loved me. I never doubted that for one minute."

"And he died in a motorcycle accident when you were seven months' pregnant?"

She blinked hard, the remembrance of that horrible time clutching at her heart. "Yes."

His eyes narrowed. "When were you married, Catherine?"

"Two weeks after you and I broke up. And before you even ask—I'll tell you. Yes, I married Jimmy suddenly, but it wasn't the way it sounds. Jimmy and I had been friends, coworkers, and, yes—even confidantes. I needed someone, and he'd always been there for me. He never let me down. Not once."

"As—as I did."

Stay back, tears. Don't come now! "I've never been sorry I married Jimmy. Our love for one another was very real, Jonah. He was a remarkable man who asked little of me. I like to think I made him as happy as he made me."

Jonah's hands fell to his sides. For a moment he said nothing. Then he reached out his hand and gave her a faint smile. "I'm sorry. I was way out of line. It's just that, when Sunni said she'd be celebrating her tenth birthday in two weeks, well, I thought maybe that one time we—you know—"

Catherine understood how he could believe he was Sunni's father. She slipped her hand into his and looked up into his face. "No, Jonah, there is no way you could be her father."

"I could be, with the timing—"

She patted his hand and forced herself to remain calm, although his accusations had distressed her. "No. You couldn't be. Remember? I said she was premature—actually, five weeks premature. We nearly lost her."

"Well, if that's true, I guess there isn't any—"

"No. Not any way at all." She felt a great sense of relief when his face smoothed out and the creases around his eyes softened.

He shrugged.

"I'm sorry you got upset over nothing."

He quietly led her back to the sofa and pulled her down beside him. They sat in silence for some time, in their own thoughts.

Finally Jonah spoke. "You know, Cat. . .after my parents had our marriage annulled, I decided I never wanted to get married. And since then I've seen so many of my college buddies get married, have a kid or two, and finally end up in a nasty divorce. I didn't want that to happen to me, so I made sure I never got that serious with anyone. Not that I had the time, with all my studies and starting a practice."

He took her hand and gave it a gentle squeeze. "Until I met Sunni, I never realized how much I'd missed by not having a wife and children. Someone to come home to at the end of a long day, to share my hopes and dreams with. You're a lucky woman, even though you are raising your daughter alone."

"If your parents hadn't convinced you to have that annulment, you and I may have had children," she reminded him gently.

He adjusted his position and stared off in space. "Yeah, you're right. They made a real mess out of our lives, didn't they? And the sad part is, I let them. Their arguments might have made sense to me back then. But in retrospect I'm not so sure I made the right decision."

"Right decision?"

"It would have been tough marrying you and paying for college, with a wife to support, trying to keep my grades up, working a full-time job, and—"

"We could've done it, Jonah. I know we could have. I told you I'd work until you finished college."

He shook his head. "To be honest, Cat, even though our plans sounded romantic and workable at the time, I was never convinced we could make it on the money you'd bring in from an entry-level job. During the first couple of years, I may have been able to hold down a part-time job and manage my studies. But after that—well, I wasn't the brightest kid on the block. I would have needed to spend all my time studying. Medical school was hard, but I'd planned on being a doctor since I was a kid, and I worked hard to get that M.D. tacked to my name. I hate to admit it, but I guess reaching my goal was more important to me at the time than you and I and the love we felt for one another. I sound pretty crass, don't I?"

"Not really." She moved closer to him to pat his shoulder. For the first time she realized what his decision to marry her could have cost him. In the long run he, too, had paid dearly to reach his goal. She wasn't the only one who had suffered. "I'm glad you told me this." Old feelings stirred within her.

"You'd always looked up to me, as if I could do anything, and I wasn't sure if I was man enough to try it alone without my parents' help. Pretty selfish, wasn't I?"

"No. I wouldn't call it selfish exactly, but I wish you'd told me all of this. It would've helped me understand—"

"Understand that I was your husband for one short evening— then allowed my parents to break us apart with their threats after I'd pledged my life to you? Before God?"

"Yes—it would have helped."

She felt his chin rest gently against her hair.

"I am so sorry, Cat. That one evening together was the most beautiful thing I've ever experienced."

She started to speak, but he silenced her.

"Let me finish. Please. I know I was your—first. You gave me the most precious thing a woman could give a man. And I felt like a heel for taking it, then leaving you. You don't know how many times during the past ten years I've thought about you and wished things could have been different for us. That I'd stood up to my parents like a man and whisked you off like the knight in shining armor you thought I was. But I didn't. I let them convince me to abandon you."

She held her breath as he spoke the words she'd ached to hear for ten long years.

"That guilt has hung over me like a heavy chain about my neck. What if you'd gotten—?"

"But I didn't."

"But you could have." He stroked the back of her hand with his thumb. "I worried about it for months. That's one of the reasons I wanted to see you that Christmas. I'd made up my mind that if you were pregnant I was going to quit school and marry you—again."

"But your parents! Your dream of becoming a doctor!"

"If I'd found out you were pregnant with our baby, I would have given it all up. Honest. I did a lot of growing up those first few months. But, thank God, you weren't, although Sunni had me worried tonight when she told me about her birthday!"

"You got upset over nothing."

He squeezed her hand. "Our parents might've thought it was puppy love, but we knew better, didn't we?"

"Yes, we did." She blinked hard, then wiped her eyes with the back of her free hand. "You were my first—"

He bent down and kissed her cheek. "You were my first, too. I know I explained that to you that night, although I wasn't sure you believed me."

"I believed you, Jonah. I always believed you. That's why it hurt so bad when we were parted so suddenly on our wedding night."

His words broke her heart. How much they'd loved one another no one but the two of them would ever know. Their love was like a fairy tale. She'd thought then, at eighteen, that she would never love a man as she did Jonah Shelton.

"I'd like to make it up to you somehow. I mean it, Cat. You name it, and if it's within my power I'll do it."

She reached out and stroked his cheek. "You don't owe me anything. It was your parents I blamed the most. I realize now that you were just a boy. And although our night together ended so quickly, I've never regretted the short time we had together as husband and wife. Not once."

"Me either. I just wish it had never ended."

She felt his breath against her cheek as he bent to kiss her forehead. She loved being close to him again, even if only for a few minutes. "I never doubted your love, Jonah. That's why the ending of our marriage nearly killed me." Her words were a mere whisper.

Her heart said, *I love you*, but he couldn't hear it.

❧

Jonah ran his fingers through his hair and let out a deep sigh as he stared at the beautiful woman sitting so close to him. He smiled to himself. For a little while he'd believed he was Sunni's father, and if he were honest he would admit he liked the idea. He was surprised at how much he enjoyed being with her. Perhaps it was because she was Cat's daughter. He'd always felt sorry for his peers who were burdened with the responsibility of caring for children and the obligation of having to spend time with them. Now he wondered if they'd felt sorry for him.

He nuzzled his chin in Catherine's hair, the feelings of love he'd buried all these years taking on new life. "I've asked God to forgive me. Can you ever forgive me, Cat?"

"I—I admit I was hurt. You've told me over and over how sorry you are for letting them end our marriage and for walking out on me. I believe you now. I forgive you."

"You forgive me? Oh, you have no idea how sweet those words sound. Or how long I've wanted to hear them. I was so foolish. You know, Cat—until I met you and fell in love with you, I didn't know what real love was. I'd never seen it before."

"But your parents—"

"My parents? That's a joke. Once, when I was about Sunni's age, I got sick at school and came home early, and there, in our own living room, was my mother with a friend of my dad's. They were kissing."

"Kissing? Your mother? That's so hard to believe."

He nodded. "Yes, my mother. I didn't know what to do, so I went back outside and hid in the yard until I saw them leave in my mother's car."

"Maybe he was just a friend."

He stiffened at the memory. "No, even at ten I could tell that was not a friendly kiss. Not the way they were going at it. His hands were all over her. I didn't realize then or even know what it was, but they were having an affair."

Catherine patted his cheek. "Poor Jonah. To experience something like that when you were so young. It must have really disturbed you."

"That wasn't the only time. By the time I was in high school, a series of strange men had been in and out of our house and, I'm sure, in and out of her bed."

Catherine stiffened. "No, Jonah! Not your mother. She was always so—prim and proper."

"She puts on a good front. I have to admit, though, that I don't know what happened after I left for college. Since I've been home, things have seemed okay."

"Didn't your father ever suspect?"

He drew in a deep breath. "Probably, but he had his own skeletons."

"Skeletons? What do you mean?"

"I think everyone but my mother knew his secretary was really his mistress. Or maybe she ignored the fact, since she liked the life he provided for her and was having her own flings."

"Oh, Jonah, I'm so sorry. I didn't know. You never told me."

"I never wanted to burden you, but now maybe you can understand why I've never married. I've been cynical. I had terrible role models. I hate to admit this to you, Cat—and please don't take it the wrong way—but I was kind of relieved when I got to college and didn't have a wife to worry about. I was sour on marriage after living with my folks. In public they were the perfect loving couple. In private they were like two strangers who lived their own lives. Oh, they were civil to one another most of the time, but I rarely saw any affection between them. It made me a skeptic. And, as much as I wanted to be with you, I was concerned about making a promise before God that I would stay married for the rest of my life. I could never live under the same roof with someone, as my mother and father did, and pretend I was happy."

"If I'd only known—"

"I'm glad you didn't. If you'd been as disillusioned with marriage as I'd been, you might not have married Jim Barton, and you wouldn't have that beautiful daughter of yours."

His lips grazed her cheek, then trailed gently toward her mouth. "You're very lucky, you know. You have Sunni in your life. What do I have?"

"You've fulfilled your dream. You've become a doctor," she said in a half whisper as his lips brushed hers. "And you're a partner in your uncle's clinic."

"And I'm involved with a woman I don't love who thinks I'm going to marry her." He backed away a bit. "It's not enough,

Cat. It's just not enough. I need"—he paused—"I–I need someone I truly love. Someone to spend my life with. I need a wife, Cat. I need children. I've finally realized—without those things—everything I've accomplished is nothing."

He reluctantly let Catherine pull herself from his arms. She rose quickly. "It's late, Jonah. I think you'd better go."

He reached out his hand, but instead of taking it she handed him his jacket.

"Sunni and I have to get up early in the morning. Sunday is the day we do our yard work. The grass needs cutting, and the flower beds need weeding. I've—I've got to get to bed. It's been a long day."

Jonah slipped his arm about her waist as they walked toward the door and was glad when she didn't protest. "Can I talk you and Sunni into going to church with me in the morning?"

He felt her body stiffen. "Church? No, thanks. We don't go to church."

He withdrew his arm and turned her toward him. "Ever?"

"Occasionally, on Christmas and Easter. That's about it."

Her answer surprised him. "But why? You're such a wonderful mother. I felt sure you attended regularly. You seem like the kind of woman who—"

"Who what?" she asked. "Who would pray and ask God for things He'd never deliver? No, thanks."

He stared at her, stunned by her words. "He does answer prayer, Cat. He answered prayer when I asked Him to help me find you!"

Her hands moved quickly to her hips. "It took him ten years to answer your prayer? That's some God! At least He answered you. That's more than He ever did for me."

"Of course it didn't take Him ten years," he shot back. "He could have answered in the twinkling of an eye if He'd wanted to. I only asked Him three months ago."

"Oh? Only three months ago? After all these years, that's

when you decided to come looking for me? What happened, Jonah? Did your conscience finally catch up with you?"

Her attitude toward God ripped at his heart, and he nearly said some flippant words he might regret later. But he held them in, remembering how much her position paralleled his own a few months earlier.

"Catherine," he said in a low, even tone, "until several months ago, I didn't even know or care if there was a God. In my eyes He'd never done anything for me. He was simply another swear word I and people around me would use. But three months ago I met an elderly woman, a cancer patient at our clinic who was facing imminent death. She introduced me to her Lord and helped me see that in God's sight I was a sinner, but that He loved me very much."

"You had one of those so-called religious experiences?" Catherine asked with a mocking tone in her voice.

"Yes, I had one of those religious experiences. I admitted to God that I was a sinner and asked for His forgiveness. Right there beside her hospital bed I turned my life over to Him, Catherine, and I haven't been the same since that day."

"That's fine for you, but as I said, God has done nothing for me. I don't need Him in my life."

He nodded his head toward Sunni's bedroom. "How about her? I'd say He's given you many blessings. Sunni alone should be enough to make you thankful."

"If He's such a good God, where was He when your parents came storming into our motel room and took you away from me? Where was He when she was born premature and nearly died? Where was He when Jimmy had that accident? I could go on and on, Jonah." She pointed a finger in his face. "And don't call me a sinner. I was a good wife, and I'm a good mother. I've worked hard to provide for both of us. God never lifted a finger to help. Don't talk to me about church. I don't need it, and neither does Sunni!"

She opened the door. Reluctantly he stepped outside.

"I've had a good time with you tonight," he said, changing the subject. "When can I see you again? Tomorrow, maybe?"

She shook her head vigorously. "No, it's been nice seeing you, too. And, believe it or not, I have enjoyed talking with you. But I have a daughter to take care of, and with my business taking most of my time, well, I think we'd better just end it here."

He moved to grab the door, but she closed it quickly, and he was left standing alone in the night.

"Women!" He jammed his fists into his jacket pockets. "Who can understand them? Lord, You probably knew best when You didn't give me one!"

❧

Catherine slammed the door then leaned against it and began to cry. All these years she'd hated Jonah and his parents for ruining her life. Now, after hearing Jonah bare his soul, she was the one who felt guilty. She, too, had been frightened by his parents' harsh, demeaning words and threats and had cowered there under the covers instead of standing up to them. She'd let them take him from her that night. Why hadn't she stood her ground? Perhaps Jonah would have been stronger if she'd challenged his parents along with him.

But what had she done to help him? Nothing. Absolutely nothing. She'd simply stayed on her side of the bed, clinging to the sheets, keeping her silence, her mouth gaping, her tears flowing like a silly teenager instead of a grown woman old enough to be married. No wonder he'd gone away so peaceably. She'd let it happen. It was as much her fault as it was his! She could have stood up to his parents and explained that both she and Jonah were of age, but she'd remained silent.

Now, after all these years, he'd turned up on her doorstep, apologizing, wanting to make amends and trying to make her and Sunni part of his life. Didn't he understand? She could never be part of his life! Not even as a friend! She would never fit in with his wealthy socialite friends, and his parents would no more accept her now than they had ten years ago. Couldn't Jonah see that?

He was a brilliant doctor. He had social obligations. He was as at home in the country club as she was at the corner supermarket. Perhaps Alexandra wasn't lying after all. Perhaps the two of them had planned to get married, and he wasn't being honest with her about it.

He'd told her about that God stuff going on in his life. Maybe his conscience had been bothering him all these years, and the only way he could soothe it was to find her and apologize. And then maybe he was just playing a game with her. Find the old girlfriend and lead her on. Pin the tail on the donkey. Pass "Go" and collect two hundred dollars.

No, there was no hope for the two of them—ever. Jonah could walk back out of her life as quickly as he'd come back in, and there would be no way to stop him. The best way to avoid being hurt again was to avoid Jonah Shelton altogether.

Her body slid into a heap on the floor, and she buried her face in her hands. Deep, uncontrollable sobs racked her body. She gathered a handful of her skirt and wiped at her eyes.

I did the right thing by sending Jonah away. I know I did. No matter how much it hurt to see him walk out of my life—again. I had to let him go.

۶۰

The next day, with a plan firmly in mind, Jonah called the hospital and was approved to perform surgery.

Next he called in the nurse who assisted on the most difficult cases.

۶۰

Catherine sat at her desk and stared blankly at the computer screen. Her life had been miserable since Saturday night. Sunni kept asking about Jonah, and he was on her mind, too. She'd learned so much about him that night. He'd exposed his very soul to her, and she'd sent him away.

When the phone rang, she let the machine pick up. She wasn't in the mood to talk to clients or anyone this morning, and she certainly wasn't ready to talk to Jonah. Not that he'd ever call again, after she'd been rude and slammed the door in his face.

"Mrs. Barton. This is Judith Bond. I'm a nurse, and I need to speak with you. You can call—"

Catherine snatched up the phone. "Has something happened to Sunni? Has she been hurt at school?"

"No, Mrs. Barton. I'm calling with good news," the woman explained. "We've set your arrival at the hospital for four in the afternoon this Thursday. Your surgery will be at seven the next morning, and—"

The young mother shifted the phone to her other ear. "My surgery? What surgery? Who did you say you were?"

nine

"My name is Judith Bond. I'm Dr. Jonah Shelton's assistant. The doctor asked me to phone you with the times and tell you the financial arrangements have been made, exactly as he'd told you when you had your consultation. Everything has been finalized, but I'll need you to come by the office and sign a few papers. He said you will probably be in the hospital no more than three or four days. Do you have any questions?"

Catherine's jaw dropped. What was happening? Why had Jonah gone to all this trouble for a woman who'd treated him so badly?

"Mrs. Barton? Are you there?"

"Yes. But there has been a mistake. I never told Dr. Shelton I was going ahead with the surgery."

"Well, Mrs. Barton, all I know is Dr. Shelton gave me strict orders, not fifteen minutes ago, to call you and give you this information. If you want to make other arrangements, I suggest you speak with him."

The screen saver on the computer came on and mooed loudly as a black-and-white cow crossed the screen. Catherine hit the volume button and spoke into the phone. "Is he there? I'd like to speak with him."

"I'm sorry, Mrs. Barton. The doctor is out of his office for the rest of the day and all day tomorrow. He performs surgery on Monday, Tuesday, and Friday. If you'd like, I can have him call you when he gets out of surgery."

Catherine touched the deep scar with her fingertips. Since the day it had happened, she'd hoped that one day she could afford to have reconstruction done on it. But from the way her finances looked, that day would never come. Now here was her chance to get it done by one of the finest reconstructive teams around—and at no cost. And she was about to turn down his amazing offer.

"I'll. . .I'll. . .when. . . ?"

"I'm not sure what time he'll be able to call. It depends on what time his last surgery is finished."

She had to quit babbling and give the woman an answer. "Wh–what if I simply cancel?"

"It's your option, Mrs. Barton. But Dr. Shelton told me that if you tried to cancel I was to tell you everyone involved in your surgery has already cleared their calendars to make room for it. He said he has the finest team available lined up, and he'd hate to have to tell them you'd cancelled."

Catherine's heart pounded wildly. Had he given her no choice in this matter? What should she do? Finally she gathered her wits about her and asked, "Ma–may I have your number, Ms. Bond? I'll call you back within the hour, I promise. I just need time to think. I was not at all prepared for this. I had no idea he was planning to do my surgery this soon."

With shaking hands, she balanced the phone on her shoulder and jotted the woman's name and number in her notebook, thanked her, and hung up.

When Jonah had said he'd wanted to repay her for all the heartache he'd caused her, she never dreamed he'd do it this way. He'd certainly taken fast action on his words.

She paced back and forth in her little office as her fingers stroked the nasty scar.

"Hey, anyone home?"

Catherine rushed into the living room and threw her arms about her sister's neck. "You have no idea how glad I am to see you!"

"Hey, you're choking me. What's got you so uptight? You

and Jonah have a fight?" Joy grinned and pulled her sister's arms from around her neck.

For the next several minutes Catherine gave her sister a nutshell version of the weekend's happenings. Joy sat on the sofa with her mouth open.

"Wow! I don't talk to you for a couple of days, and lightning strikes. You've had some weekend. How's the kid taking it?"

Catherine frowned, threw herself back onto the sofa's soft cushions, and propped her feet on the coffee table, something she rarely allowed herself or her daughter to do. "Not good. She's crazy about the guy. You should see the two of them together."

"You can't blame her for latching on to him. Not with the way he's been treating her. You're a great mom, but you'll never take the place of a dad. That's what she's looking for, a father image. I guess all girls her age need and want that."

"Well, if slamming the door in his face got my message across, he's out of her life now. Out of both of our lives. But what do I do about the surgery?"

Joy picked up a mint from the candy dish on the table and popped it into her mouth. "Surgery? What do you mean?"

"That's what I was about to tell you. Remember when I told you Jonah offered to repair my scar?"

"Yes!"

Catherine explained about the nurse's call while Joy's mouth gaped open again. "I told her I'd call her within the hour."

Her sister leaned toward her. "You're going to do it, aren't you? You'll never be able to afford it otherwise, unless you win the lottery—and since you never buy any tickets, your odds aren't too great."

Catherine smiled wistfully as she touched the scar. "I know I'd feel better about myself if I had it done. And I'd trust Jonah with my life. I'm not worried about the surgery."

Joy jumped to her feet and pulled her sister up with her.

"Then do it. Go to the phone and call that nurse and tell her you'll be there."

"You really think I should? Under the circumstances?"

Joy gave her a sisterly pat on the arm. "Under the circumstances? You mean since Jonah wants to do this badly enough he went to all this trouble to set it up for you? Yes, I'd say under those circumstances you'd be an idiot to say no. I'll take care of the kid for you, so you can't use her as an excuse. Go! Call!" She shoved Catherine toward her office. "Now!"

❧

Jonah listened in on the extension as the nurse spoke with Catherine. Then he gave her a thumbs-up after she ended the conversation. "Good job. Thanks. We pulled it off."

"I hope so. As you could tell, it took a little persuading."

"I'm not surprised. She's a proud woman. She's been taking care of her daughter and herself for a number of years without anyone's help. But I figured she'd come around. She hates that scar."

The nurse gave him a dubious look. "What are you up to, Jonah? Who is this woman anyway? I've never heard you mention her, and to my knowledge she's never been in here as a patient. I felt like an actor in an old spy movie, talking to her like that."

"Long story, Judith. Let's just say I owe this woman, and I want to repay an old debt. A ten-year-old debt."

"Debt? Does she have any idea what an operation like this would cost her if she had to pay for it?"

"I think she has a fair idea. That's why it was difficult for her to refuse."

She shrugged. "Whatever you say, but I have a feeling there's a great deal more to this story than you're willing to tell me. But it's your party. Invite whomever you wish."

As soon as she left his office, he thanked God for answered prayer. Next he called the florist.

❧

Catherine stared at the calendar on her desk, mumbling to herself. Thursday afternoon. That only gave her a couple of days to complete her work, make arrangements with her clients, and do a myriad of other things.

She flipped the calendar page. "Sunni has a dental checkup scheduled for Monday," she said. "I'll have to call and reschedule. Then there's the grade conference at Sunni's school a week from Thursday." She squeezed her face between her hands. "What am I thinking? I can't possibly have surgery now."

But deep within a voice whispered, *Don't you want to get rid of that scar? You've got to have this surgery.*

"But having the operation will mean spending time around Jonah," she reminded that voice aloud. "I'm not sure I can handle it."

You handled it ten years ago, the voice countered. *You can do it again. You're much stronger than you were then, and you have Sunni now. He wants to do this, or he wouldn't have gone to so much trouble to set it up for you.*

She sighed.

❧

When the doorbell rang late that afternoon, Catherine grumbled to herself. She hit the save button on her computer, slipped on her shoes, and hurried to answer it.

"Catherine Hayley-Barton?"

She eyed the long white box in the young woman's arms, then looked past her to the minivan parked in the driveway. The words Village Florist were painted in big letters on the side. "Yes, I'm Catherine Barton."

"Then these are for you. Be sure to put them in water as soon as you open them, if you want them to last."

She pushed open the storm door and took the box from the delivery girl's hands. Who would be sending her flowers? Her birthday was months away, and she couldn't remember any other occasion. She untied the red satin ribbon and lifted the lid cautiously. One dozen perfectly formed, wonderfully scented, red roses lay inside on a bed of green tissue paper.

She lowered her face and breathed in the lovely fragrance ,then set the lid aside and picked up the little white envelope that lay on top of the beautiful roses. She stared at it. She couldn't remember ever receiving a dozen long-stemmed roses. No one in her life would have sent them to her. Her parents couldn't afford it, her sisters wouldn't do such a thing, and Jimmy had been much too frugal to spend his hard-earned money on flowers that would wilt and die. They couldn't be from her daughter. Sunni was much too young to have that kind of money.

She removed the card and read: *Don't worry. We're going to take good care of you.* It was signed: *Dr. Jonah Shelton and your surgical team.*

Catherine hugged the little card to her heart. The dream of a lifetime was finally coming true. She was going to get rid of the horrible scar, the constant reminder of that frightful night when Jonah was taken away from her.

⁂

It was all Jonah could do to keep from phoning Catherine; yet he knew that if he called her it would give her a chance to change her mind. He had to make sure that didn't happen. Normally he and his Uncle Bert would have several appointments with a patient before performing an operation of this magnitude. But staying away from her until she was settled into her room at the hospital was no doubt the best way to handle things. He'd had an opportunity to study the scar several times already, and he'd make certain he and his uncle Bert would go over the final details with the surgical team after she was admitted to the hospital on Thursday.

At last he'd found a means to repay her, and if he had his way this surgery would also keep him in Catherine's and Sunni's lives.

❧

For Catherine, Thursday arrived all too soon. She'd had so many details to take care of in such a short time, but she'd made it. She had checked off everything on her to-do list.

She unpacked her suitcase and looked around the sterile room, smiling. This was the first time she'd been in a hospital since Sunni was born. "What am I doing here? I've lived with this scar all these years. Am I being vain wanting to have it fixed?" She stared into the mirror on the wall above the vanity.

No, you're not vain. You're still young. You have the best part of your life ahead of you, that inner voice assured her. *Sunni wants you to have it done, too. Remember how excited she was when she heard you were going through with the operation? Do it, not only for yourself, but for her.*

She slipped into her gown, the pink lace one, one of three Sunni had insisted she buy for her hospital stay.

"You can't wear those awful faded pajamas!" Sunni had told her. The girl had even offered her money to buy new ones from funds she'd been saving for summer camp.

Catherine hung the few clothes she'd brought in the little closet and placed her personal belongings in the drawers, then pulled a magazine from her purse and slipped beneath the white sheets. The volunteer who'd escorted her to the room had told her supper would be arriving soon, but since she was scheduled for early morning surgery it wouldn't be much.

She'd barely started reading an article on business management when she heard the door open. Assuming it was supper, she closed her magazine, placed it on the nightstand, and folded her hands.

"Mrs. Barton? I'm Dr. Shelton, Jonah Shelton. My uncle, Dr. Bert Shelton, and I will be doing your reconstructive surgery in the morning. I need to ask you a few questions and examine that scar."

Catherine sat up quickly and pulled the sheet around her.

Wordlessly she watched as Jonah, in his professional stance, circled her bed with a clipboard in his hand.

"I'd prefer you have no liquids after ten o'clock tonight, and go easy on your supper tray when it comes. The less you have in your stomach, the easier it will be on you in recovery."

His eyes continued to scan the clipboard.

"Someone will awaken you about five in the morning and take you to pre op, where you'll be prepared for surgery. I'll be in early, so if any questions come to you between now and then, we can discuss them at that time."

He laid the clipboard calmly on the bed and pulled a small flashlight from his pocket. "Now let's have another look at that scar."

She felt his hand touch her chin firmly as he tilted her head to one side. He was so close she could feel his breath on her cheek.

"Uh-huh. Yes, just as I thought. Uh-huh."

She tried not to move and allowed his hands to determine the position of her head as he probed the scar with his fingertips.

"Yes, we'll be able to smooth that out quite nicely. The only place we may have any difficulty is this area in your hairline. But, considering its location, I don't think you'll even realize it's there, once the surgery is completed."

She watched him slip the flashlight back into his pocket, then jot a number of notes on his clipboard. He was totally professional. She'd never seen him in this setting. His demeanor exuded confidence, and she knew she was in good hands.

"You may be a little nauseated when the anesthetic begins to wear off, but other than that you should be fairly comfortable. I'll prescribe some pain medication, but I'd prefer you not take it unless you really need it. You can plan on going home Tuesday. Other than resting several hours a day, you should be able to resume your work at home. I'll have my nurse set up your first follow-up appointment. And, yes,

Sunni can visit you as soon as you feel up to it. Probably by Friday evening. Any questions?"

She shook her head. She couldn't think of one. He'd answered them all.

"Fine. Be expecting several other members of my team to look in on you this evening. They'll want to have a good look at that scar. Don't worry, and try to get a good night's sleep. I'll see you in the morning, and we'll get to work on that pretty face of yours." He took her hand in his. "Good night, Mrs. Barton."

Still speechless, she watched him walk out the door and close it softly behind him.

She realized she hadn't said one word.

&

Catherine opened her eyes and tried to look about the room. She blinked several times to clear the fuzziness that blurred her vision. Her mouth felt the way spoiled food smelled. The left side of her head and neck was numb. She lifted her hand to touch them but felt only a huge blob of gauze and tape.

"How do you feel, Sis?"

She hadn't realized Joy was standing beside her bed. Still unable to focus, she mumbled through lips that refused to move. "It–it's. . .over?" Her voice sounded as fuzzy to her as the room appeared.

Joy bent and kissed her sister's good cheek. "Yes, all over. Jonah said you did fine. He's very happy with the results."

"Jonah?" She wished the room would stand still instead of shifting back and forth. It was making her dizzy.

"Oh, yes. He's been at your side all morning. He just went to check on a couple of patients who'd been asking for him. He'll be back in a little while." Joy patted her hand again.

"Where's Sunni?"

"With Mom and Dad. I'm going to pick her up later and bring her to see you. Jonah said it'd be okay."

"Didn't talk to him."

Her voice was so soft that her sister had to lean close to understand her. "What do you mean? You didn't talk to him?"

Catherine blinked again. Her face felt as if it were being squeezed by a vise. Not painful, just uncomfortable. "When he came. . .hospital. . .didn't say. . .word."

Joy smiled. "Maybe he was trying to make it easier on you. He knew you'd feel peculiar after shoving him out the door last weekend."

Catherine tried to smile, but her face wouldn't cooperate. "I'm sl–sleepy, Jo–Joy."

Joy kissed the tip of her finger, then touched her finger to one of the few spots on her sister's face that wasn't covered by the bandage. "Then sleep, Kiddo. It'll do you good."

❧

By Saturday morning Catherine was feeling more like herself. When Dr. Jonah Shelton made his early morning visit, he told her she could start walking around the corridor to get some exercise. He was still calling her Mrs. Barton and maintaining his professional stance, treating her as he would any other patient. She began to wonder if she would ever again see the Jonah she had known.

After his visit she slipped into her robe, donned her slippers, and began her walk around the big outer circle of hallways. It felt good to move around again, even though her legs felt rubbery. She was not used to staying in bed.

She'd made the round once and was starting a second time when the elevator doors opened and the last woman in the world she wanted to see stepped out.

Eldora Shelton.

Catherine tried to step around the woman, hoping she wouldn't recognize her with all the years that had passed and her face bandaged.

But the woman caught her by the arm and said sharply, "Catherine, I have some things to say to you. Now."

ten

Mystified by both her sudden appearance and her words, Catherine stared at the woman. Why would Eldora Shelton come to see her? How did she know she was there? "Ah—I guess we can sit over there on those chairs near the nurses' station."

The two cautiously sat down beside one another, maintaining a good distance between them. Eldora glanced around, as if to make sure their conversation wasn't being overheard. "You are nothing but a gold digger." Her eyes flashed with contempt and anger.

"How can you say that? I've done nothing to you or to Jonah! It's been ten years since I've even seen him!"

Eldora grabbed Catherine's wrist so tightly she wanted to cry out. "I've come to warn you to stay away from my son. You nearly ruined his life once, and you are not going to do it again!" Her words were direct. Harsh.

Catherine couldn't believe what she was hearing. "Me? The last thing I'd want to do is hurt Jonah!"

"I know better, Catherine. Alexandra said you've been stalking him. Inviting him to your home, and now you've hired him to do this surgery on some ridiculously small scar. Couldn't you think of a better excuse to be around him than to have him do some meaningless cosmetic surgery to improve your looks?"

Catherine gasped. Her hands moved quickly to hold her head. "Small cosmetic surgery? Nearly my entire head is bandaged, and you call this a small cosmetic surgery?" She wasn't sure if it was time for her pain pill, or if the woman seated beside her had caused this sudden onrush of pain, but either way her head was pounding.

Eldora rose to her feet, stuffed her big purse under her arm, and pointed her finger in Catherine's face. "You stay out of my son's life, or you'll pay dearly. I mean it. He's going to marry Alexandra."

Despite the woozy feelings in her head, Catherine stood and faced her. "That sounds like a threat, Mrs. Shelton. I hope this time Jonah makes up his own mind and doesn't listen to you and your husband."

The red-faced woman leaned toward her angrily. "It is a threat, and you'd better be smart enough to take it that way. You have no idea of the power the Sheltons have in this town. We'll ruin you. That's a promise!"

Catherine watched Eldora Shelton swirl around and march over to the elevators, arriving in time to step into one before the door closed behind her. *How can such a hateful woman have such a caring son?*

Catherine made her way back to her room and collapsed onto her bed, shaken and trembling, fearful of what the overbearing Eldora Shelton might do if she felt justified.

❧

When Dr. Jonah Shelton came in Sunday morning, he was as businesslike as he'd been the previous three days. Catherine felt as if she were talking to a stranger. But in light of his mother's visit she decided that keeping their relationship on a professional basis would be the best thing for all of them.

"You're doing fine, Mrs. Barton," he said in an impersonal tone, lifting the bandage and examining his handiwork. "Ah, it's doing very nicely. You're going to be happy with the results."

She watched him jot more notes on her chart. He was extremely handsome in his camel slacks and navy polo shirt. Probably on his way to the country club for brunch, she concluded. She liked the way he kept his hair cropped short now.

She wondered if his mother had said anything to him about her visit. Probably not.

"Well, I'll check on you tomorrow. I have several surgeries scheduled, so I'm not sure what time it will be, but if things look good you can go home Tuesday morning."

Catherine tried to contain her excitement. She'd never expected to go home this soon. "Good," she said, struggling to keep her voice level. "It'll be nice to get home."

"I'm sure it will." He gave her a half-salute and headed for the door. "Have a nice day, Mrs. Barton."

"Uh, you, too, Dr. Shelton."

٭

Jonah let loose with an exuberant chuckle as he closed the door to Catherine's room. She was responding just as he'd hoped she would, even though it was taking every ounce of strength he could muster to keep from pulling her into his arms and kissing her.

It was nearly ten before Jonah got home Sunday night. He'd spent much of the day at his clinic going over résumés of doctors he and his partners were considering adding to their staff. He was heading for the kitchen to get a glass of milk when his mother came down the stairs.

"Hey, Mother, one of my associates told me they saw you at the hospital yesterday. One of your friends sick?"

She gave him a portentous glance. "Ah—yes. Ma—Mary. I don't think you've met her. She—she has some kind of stomach condition."

Jonah frowned. "Stomach condition? And she's the only one you went to see? Who's her doctor?"

She lifted her chin defiantly. "Of course she's the only one I went to see. Why do you ask? Since when are you concerned where I go and whom I see?"

He took one step closer. "If she has a stomach condition and she was the only one you went to visit, what were you doing up on the surgical floor? That's where you were spotted."

She turned to go, but he put his hand on her arm.

"Okay, Mother. I want an answer right now—and don't give me any of your lies. I might have believed them when I was a kid, but I'm older now, and I want the truth." His words had a sharp, commanding edge to them.

His mother tried to step away, but he held her.

"I—ah—I was looking for you."

He released his hand and shook his head sadly. Lying seemed to come so easily for her. But this time her face betrayed her.

"Fess up, Mother. Alexandra let slip that she told you I'd be operating on Catherine's face Friday. You knew she'd be on the surgical floor, didn't you? Surely you didn't go see her. What could you possibly have to say to her?"

The woman stepped back with a mortified look. Her diamond-laden hand rose and flattened against her chest. "Did someone tell you I did? If they did, they were lying!"

Jonah rubbed his forehead wearily. "No one had to tell me, Mother. You just did. Your face says it all."

"That woman is nothing but a cheap, fortune-hungry opportunist. I told you when you were in high school that the girl was up to no good. I'm sure she doesn't have any money to pay for that kind of surgery. Did she talk you into taking her on as a charity case?"

His defense mechanism kicked into high gear at the sound of her angry, misplaced words. "You have a lot of room to talk, Mother. But I won't go into that now. Let's just say it's an understatement to mention you had a few undesirable things going on in your own private life when I was a kid. Things that make Catherine look like a saint."

The woman shook her finger in her son's face. "Don't you talk to me like that, young man. I am your mother! I merely told that girl—" She stopped midsentence.

His brows lifted at her words. "Oh, so you did go to see her!"

She smoothed her sleeves then looked away. "Yes. But I did it for your own good. I simply told her you and Alexandra are going to be married and warned her—"

He pounded his fist on the end table. "Alexandra and I are going to be married? That's news to me! I don't love that woman—why would I want to marry her? And you warned Catherine? You warned her of what, Mother? To stay away from me? Is that what you did?"

He'd never talked to his mother like that. Ever. But now he wondered if he should have stood up to the woman years ago. Perhaps if he had he would be married to the only woman he'd ever loved.

She cringed slightly then straightened, taking on her customary regal stance. "You'd better not let Alexandra get away from you, Jonah. She's the perfect wife for you."

He snorted. "As I told Dad, she might be right for the two of you, but I'll pick my own wife, thank you. You might as well know that if Catherine would have me I'd marry her right now!"

He couldn't believe what he'd just said. The words had tumbled out on their own accord. Or had they? Had the girl he'd once given up so easily penetrated his protective wall of self-sufficiency and independence? Was he finally admitting to himself he'd never stopped loving Catherine?

"Jonah! How dare you even consider bringing that little nobody into the Shelton family? You'd shame us all!"

"No more than you and Father have done with your tawdry affairs!" He walked out of the room, leaving his mother speechless.

❧

Jonah stopped in to check on his patient about noon Monday, garbed in his green operating gear. "I've signed your release papers, and you're free to go home tomorrow. I'm sure Nurse Bond told you how to take care of your incision. Just follow her instructions, and you'll do fine. I'll expect to see you in my office on Thursday. Meanwhile, Mrs. Barton, take your pain pills only if you need them, and call me if you have any problems."

Wide-eyed, Catherine watched him go. What was he doing? Why was he treating her like this? Like a complete stranger? Perhaps because she'd asked for it.

The nurse lingered behind to plump her pillows. "You're a mighty lucky woman to have Dr. Shelton do your surgery, Mrs. Barton."

"I know. I've heard he has a wonderful professional reputation." Catherine bent forward and allowed the nurse to slip the pillows behind her back.

"We're mighty fortunate Dr. Shelton and his uncle decided to open this clinic in Dallas. He has a long list of patients waiting to see him. How long did you have to wait?"

Catherine leaned back and pulled the sheet about her, realizing for the first time that Jonah had given her priority over his other patients. "Not—not too long. Dr. Shelton and I are old friends." Her heart said, *Friends? That's not quite true. You've been married to the good doctor.* She wondered how the nurse would respond if she let her in on that little secret.

"Well, Mrs. Barton. Just do as Dr. Shelton says, and you'll be surprised at the results. It seems he and his uncle can work miracles. They make quite a team."

Catherine mulled over the woman's words long after she'd left the room. *He and his uncle can work miracles.* Those words caused her to wonder if they'd stayed married, would Jonah have been able to complete his studies and his internship and become a competent surgeon? The answer to that question she'd never know. But one thing was certain. The world was a better place with Dr. Jonah Shelton being part of it.

❧

Wednesday morning Jonah arrived at the office of Dallas's leading newspaper and went directly to the paper's morgue, where he was greeted by a friend he'd met during his college days. The man was now one of the paper's editors.

"I have an hour, Cliff, before my next appointment, so I'd appreciate any help you can give me."

The man shook his friend's hand then led him to a row of computers. "I told one of the men in this department what you're looking for, and he's pulled up the dates you mentioned. Let's see if he's found anything."

When the other man saw him, he extended his hand. "I'm sorry, Dr. Shelton. I didn't find what you were looking for, and I searched every issue of that year's papers. I hate to disappoint you, but there just wasn't a marriage license listed for the names you gave us."

Jonah thanked the man then walked to the lobby with his friend.

"Sorry to waste your time like that, Jonah. But that guy is good. If there'd been anything there, he would've found it. Are you sure you had the right dates and the right names?"

Jonah nodded. "Oh, yes. The information I gave you was correct. To be honest I didn't expect him to find anything. I just had to be sure."

The man scratched his head. "I don't get it. But if you're satisfied I guess that's all that counts."

Jonah thanked the man and headed back to his office.

So, Cat, how are you going to explain this?

❧

Catherine arrived at the clinic on time but was told Dr. Shelton was running slightly behind. She seated herself near the receptionist's desk and began to thumb idly through a magazine. Then she noticed the bandage on the hand of the man seated next to her. "Is your hand doing okay?" she asked when she realized he saw her watching him.

He took his good hand and carefully lifted the injured one. "Oh, yes. It's doing fine now. If it weren't for Dr. Shelton, I wouldn't have a hand, at least not a usable one."

Her eyes widened. "Really? What happened?"

"I work third shift at a machine shop. The safety guard had been removed on a machine I work on sometimes. My sleeve got caught in the gears and pulled my hand into the conveyor belt. They rushed me to the hospital and called Dr. Bert Shelton. He and that nephew of his came and spent most of the night putting my hand back together."

"They did?"

"Sure did. Me and my wife think those men were sent by God. They do your face?" the man asked with interest.

She nodded, still mulling over his words of praise for Jonah. "Yes, I have to admit I was a little leery of the operation."

"With them doing the operation you have no worries. You'll be fine, too."

When the nurse called her name, she excused herself and was ushered into one of the examination rooms. Within seconds the door opened, and Jonah appeared with her chart.

"Well, Mrs. Barton, how is that skin graft getting along? Has it given you much pain?" He tilted her head to one side, carefully pulled off the bandages, then handed her a mirror. "Don't be alarmed. It's still pretty red and bruised, but in a few weeks you'll hardly know anything was ever there."

Catherine took the mirror and gazed at the area along her jawline. A lump rose in her throat, and she fought back tears of joy. Yes, the redness and bruising were there, but the hideous scar was gone.

Impulsively she threw her arms around Jonah's neck and began to weep. "I've carried that awful scar for ten years, and in one day you've changed my life."

"Uncle Bert did most of it. Bert and God. I just assisted."

She leaned into him as his arms circled her, and he drew her close. "Oh, Jonah. How can I ever thank you?"

"Do you mean that?" he asked softly, still holding her.

"You'd do something if I asked you to?"

She pushed away slightly and looked into his face as tears of joy rolled down her cheeks. "Yes, of course. If I can."

His finger carefully brushed a tear away from the reddened, tender skin. "I'm not sure if all that salt water is good for your graft."

She smiled. She loved his sense of humor.

Then his face became serious. "As I asked you before—let me be part of Sunni's life."

eleven

Catherine froze. Jonah? Be part of her daughter's life? Why would he ask such a thing? Was it that important to him?

"Cat? You said anything," he reminded her as he continued to hold her in his arms.

"But—"

"But?"

She bit her lower lip. "Could you explain what you mean? Part? How large a part? And why?"

His hands moved to her shoulders, and he looked her squarely in the eye.

"You know. Play ball with her. Take her to a hockey game now and then. Movies. Go out for pizza. That sort of thing. And I'm sure I'd be good at helping her with her homework. I'm a college grad, remember?"

"But why? Your life is so busy. Why would you want to do such a thing?" Her mind whizzed through the group of activities he'd mentioned.

He hesitated. "She's a great kid. And I think I'd be good for her."

"But why?" she repeated. "You're so busy with the clinic, and then there's Alexandra. What would she think?"

He took a deep breath and let it out slowly. "You let me worry about Alexandra. And, as far as the time goes, most of the doctors I know play golf once or twice a week and maybe even racquetball or tennis. I've been so busy I haven't gotten involved in anything other than my practice. I've decided I need something in my life besides medicine, and I want it to be Sunni. I'll make the time. I promise."

Catherine clenched and unclenched her fists and stared at this man who had done so much for her. "I'm not sure it would be wise. For Sunni's sake. Why would you want to do such a thing when you could be playing golf or some other sport with your doctor friends? You told me yourself you never wanted a family. Or children."

He grinned. "Ah, but that was before I met Sunni. If all kids were like your daughter, I'd want a dozen."

"Well—I—you—"

"You said you'd grant me anything. Remember?"

Her common sense told her to be careful. Both she and her daughter could be hurt by such an arrangement. Having a father image in her life for a short time could be worse on Sunni than having none at all. Her heart said to go ahead and grant his request; he'd never purposely hurt either of them.

"I—I guess it'll be okay," she said reluctantly, "if you're sure that's what you want." Was she making the right decision? But under the circumstances what other answer could she give him? He'd just performed a miracle for her.

He bent his face close to hers. Close enough so she could see the flecks of gold in his deep-set eyes. "You won't be sorry, Cat." He tilted his head slightly and placed a light kiss on her lips, then murmured, "You can come with us anytime you want."

For that one moment she was eighteen again, sharing a kiss with the man she loved. The man she planned to marry. And all she wanted to do was throw her arms around his neck and kiss him with the passion of a teenager in love. Why, oh, why had their course in life been so drastically altered that night?

The two parted quickly at the sound of the door opening.

Catherine straightened, and Jonah adjusted his lab coat as Nurse Bond entered the room.

"Here's the cream you wanted for Mrs. Barton, Dr. Shelton."

She handed him the jar, then walked over to Catherine to examine her face. "Oh, my. What an improvement. They did a good job as usual. Dr. Jonah sure knows how to give his patients exactly what they need." She raised a brow and smiled mischievously, then backed out the door. But before closing it she gave them a wink and added, "Carry on with whatever you were doing."

Jonah chuckled. "Guess she saw us."

Catherine laughed, too. She was still feeling like that teenager. This was as bad as being caught and reprimanded by the school principal for kissing Jonah in the hallway. She was sure he was remembering that same incident and how embarrassed they'd both been.

Jonah cleared his throat and attempted to put on his professional face again, but the smile shone through. "Well, Mrs. Barton, it's settled. As I understand it, we've come to an agreement. Tell your daughter she can expect to hear from me this evening." He tapped the tip of her nose, then added with a grin, "As for you, you're doing fine. I want you to use that cream several times a day on that graft."

She frowned. "How much should I apply? And should I—?"

He slid his finger to her lips then traced their perimeter as he gazed into her eyes. "This doctor plans on making a house call tonight. He needs to show his patient firsthand how to apply that cream."

"But—"

He picked up her chart and opened the door. "See you at seven. Don't eat first. The doctor will be bringing pizza."

The door closed behind him.

❧

Sunni raced to the door when she heard Jonah's car in the driveway. "Mom, he's here!"

Catherine smoothed her hair as best she could. It was difficult to keep her shoulder-length hair off the bandage, but she'd managed to fasten it with a long spring-type clip. At least she could comb the hair on her good side. She smiled at her image in the mirror. She looked like the victim in a horror movie all bandaged up that way. But Jonah had said it wouldn't be for long. A quick freshening of her lipstick and a spritz of perfume, and she was ready to join her daughter and her doctor in the living room.

Jonah stood when she entered the room, and she felt like a queen. It was nice to have a man around who knew how to treat someone like a lady.

"Pizza man," he announced proudly, gesturing toward the big box on the coffee table.

Sunni leaped from her chair and ran to stand beside him. "He brought the kind I like, Mama. Wasn't that nice?"

Her mother smiled. "Very nice, Sunni. I'll get us some plates and napkins, and we can eat it in here. Is that okay with you guys?"

"Only if I can help you," Jonah said.

She felt as if she were on display as Jonah's eyes scanned her from head to toe. She was glad she'd worn the black jeans Sunni had suggested.

He followed her into the kitchen. "What do you want me to do?"

"Here—fill these." She pointed to the glasses then reached into the refrigerator and pulled out a tray of cubes and handed them to him. "The tea pitcher is on the counter."

She added plates, silverware, and napkins to a tray and watched the hands that were so skilled with tiny surgical instruments struggle to get the ice cubes out of the plastic tray. "Just give the tray a slight twist," she suggested, smiling.

He did as instructed, and little cubes of ice dropped out onto the countertop. He looked first to see if she was watching, then with a helpless shrug began picking them up and dropping them into the glasses. "Pretty clumsy, huh? The refrigerator in my parents' home spits out the ice cubes for you."

"Sorry. You have to do mine the old-fashioned way."

She liked him in blue jeans. But she liked him in the Armani suits, too. And he looked great in his surgical garb. She tried to will it to settle down, but her heart did a cartwheel. The old spark was there. Even Eldora Shelton's harsh words couldn't extinguish it.

"What else, Cat?" He filled the tray with water from the sink and dripped it all the way back to the refrigerator.

She noticed but thought better of saying anything and smiled instead. "That's it. Let's eat."

Sunni was sitting cross-legged on the center cushion of the sofa, watching TV, waiting for her pizza. Jonah put the tray on the coffee table. "I'd like to pray first—if it's okay with you two." He shot a questioning look toward Cat.

Catherine reached one hand out to her daughter and the other to Jonah. "It's fine."

The three held hands and bowed their heads. Jonah offered a simple prayer and ended it with, "And, God, we thank You for the pizza. Amen."

Sunni covered her mouth and giggled. "You think God wants to hear you talk about pizza?"

Jonah smiled confidently. "I know He does, Sunni. God is interested in everything in our lives. Even pizza. Sometime I'll show you some verses in my Bible about prayer. Would you like to see them?"

She nodded. "Sure. Some of my friends pray before their meals at school. Maybe Mom and I can go to church with you sometime."

Jonah grinned and glanced sideways at her mother. "I'd like that."

The three enjoyed the pizza and one another's company, and all too soon it was Sunni's bedtime.

"Let me know when you're ready to turn out the light,

Honey, and I'll come and tuck you in." Catherine quietly watched her daughter give Jonah a good-night hug.

"Hey, Kiddo," he said after looking at Catherine, "how about letting me tuck you in tonight?"

Catherine's expression sobered. Tucking her daughter in was something she had done every night since Sunni's birth.

But, much to her dismay, Sunni jumped at his offer. "Sure, Dr. Shelton. That'd be nice, but you've got to read me a story, like Mom always does."

Jonah gulped. "A story, huh? I probably won't be as good at it as your mom."

Sunni giggled again. "That's okay. I'll help you with the hard words."

Jonah did a quick doubletake, then grabbed the girl and hugged her to him as he roared with laughter. "Oh, you will, will you?"

Catherine watched from her place on the couch and wondered how she could have such feelings of elation and feelings of dread at the same time. It was good to see Sunni so happy; yet she imagined her daughter slipping away from her, and she didn't like the feeling.

Five minutes later, when Sunni called out from her room that she was ready to be tucked in, Jonah stood up quickly with a grin. "I'm not sure I'm up to this, but—"

"I'll do it!"

He shook his head. "No, I want to do it. It's just that I've never done anything like this before, and I'm kind of scared."

Catherine chuckled. "The big doctor is scared of reading a story to a ten-year-old girl?"

"No, not that," he said with a mischievous grin. "Afraid I'll really have to ask her to help me with the hard words."

She tossed one of the sofa's small cushions at him then smiled. "You'll do fine."

"You'll come to my rescue if I holler for help?"

"Of course I will."

She watched until he disappeared into Sunni's open doorway. Soon their sounds of laughter came floating down the hall, and she knew Jonah must be reading the story as he'd promised.

Catherine picked up the cushion from the floor where it had fallen, settled herself in the corner of the sofa, slipped off her shoes, and put her feet on the edge of the coffee table. She had to admit it was nice having Jonah around, but his fascination with her daughter frightened her. What was his real motive for wanting to spend time with Sunni? Surely he still didn't think Sunni was his daughter when she'd done everything she could think of to convince him otherwise.

"Hey, you should've heard me. I was pretty good. At least your daughter thought I was." He dropped down on the sofa beside her and scooted close. "Those books of hers are pretty interesting."

She gave an exaggerated pat to his arm. "I'm sure you were very good. Anyone who can pronounce those medical terms you wrestle with every day should be able to deal with children's books."

He beamed, apparently pleased by her confidence in his abilities. "She invited me to come and watch her softball game tomorrow afternoon after school. I told her I would. Is that okay with you?"

She paused. He sure hadn't wasted any time working his way into Sunni's life. "I guess, but can you get away at that time of day?" She was aware of the heavy load he carried.

"Hey, that's the advantage of having a junior doctor following around at your heels. I'll just assign him to a couple of my understanding patients. They won't mind a bit, and he'll jump at the chance for the experience."

He leaned back and spread his arms across the back of the sofa. "You know, this is nice. I've never spent an evening like this before. Sure beats attending that black-tie affair."

Catherine edged closer. "You were supposed to attend a black-tie event tonight?"

He rested his head against the back of the sofa and reached for her hand. "Uh-huh. With Alexandra and my parents. Some fund-raising thing for a music theater, I think. Or maybe it was the ballet. One of my mother's pet projects. I don't remember which."

Catherine shifted her position and tried to put the conversation she'd had with Mrs. Shelton out of her mind. She wondered if the woman's circle of friends had any idea what a vindictive person she really was.

"You do remember my mother, don't you, Cat?"

His voice held a certain inflection in it; she suspected he meant something else by his question. "Yes, of course I remember her."

"Have you seen her lately?"

Her body went rigid.

"You weren't going to tell me about her visit, were you?"

She let out a sigh. "No, I wasn't," she said timidly.

He lifted his arm and put it around her shoulders. "I've warned her to stay away from you."

"And she warned me to stay away from you! She—" She bit her lip to keep the words from escaping. "Never mind."

His arm tightened about her. "She what?"

"She said you were engaged, and—"

He scowled. "I'm not, Cat! I'm still dating Alexandra now and then, mostly to please my parents, but we are not getting married. I've already told you that."

"But she said—"

"Who are you going to believe? Me or my mother?"

"You, I guess."

He relaxed his grip, then gave her a slight squeeze. "I don't want to ruin our evening by talking about my parents and

Alexandra. Could you get that jar of cream for me? I want to show you how to apply it."

She welcomed the change of subject and hurried to her room to retrieve the jar.

He pulled out the straight-backed chair from the little desk and motioned for her to be seated. "I'm going to take those bandages off. You won't be needing them anymore."

Not needing them anymore? She wanted to shout for joy. She thought she'd be wearing them for at least another week.

He removed the tape and the gauze, examined the area, then unscrewed the lid from the jar, and began gently applying the silky smooth cream to her face. "Have you had a chance to see what I had to do to your hair?"

"No, I haven't. Only the part you showed me at the hospital."

"I had to shave out about a two-inch square just above your ear, but it should all grow back in no time. You might have a little trouble finding a suitable hairstyle until then." He stuck the tip of one finger into the jar. "I guess you could get a job as a rock star in the meantime. They'd like that jazzy haircut. Can you play the guitar?"

She smiled up at him. The cream on his fingertips felt cool, yet soothing, as he worked it into her skin. The area wasn't nearly as sensitive as she'd expected it to be.

"It still has a lot of redness there, especially on this area here in front of your ear, where the scar made a slight turn. But it'll leave soon—don't be too concerned. Does any of this hurt?"

She gave her head a light shake.

"Good. Then just relax, close your eyes, and let me rub this cream in. The massaging is good for it. It should be done several times a day."

She did as she was told.

His fingers moved smoothly over her upper neck and jaw-line in small circular motions, working their way slowly into her hairline and across her scalp. "Doing okay?" he asked with a hushed voice.

"Fine," she whispered.

"I'm not hurting you?" He continued to massage the area.

"Umm," she murmured, enjoying each touch of his hand. "I feel like purring."

"Just relax. I want to apply another coating."

His fingers continued to work their magic, and she felt like a glob of clay in an artist's hand.

Suddenly she felt his lips on hers. Touching then pressing gently. "We can't, Jonah," she stated flatly as she came to her senses and turned her head away.

He seemed puzzled. "Why? We're both single adults. What's to stop us?"

"The little girl sleeping in there, for one," she said almost apologetically as she pointed toward the hallway.

"I don't see her objecting to us being together. In fact, I think she kinda likes it."

"Alexandra."

"I've already told you—we're only dating, and not at all these days."

"Your parents."

"Hey, I'm a grown man. They can't threaten to take my college money away from me anymore."

"You."

"What do you mean? Me. I'm all for getting to know you again. Nothing would please me more."

She moved to the sofa and covered her face with her hands. "You're from a different world than mine. You always have been."

❧

He dropped down beside her. "I'm not proposing we spend our lives together, although that might not be such a bad idea. I'm only asking you to let us spend time together, get to know one another again. Have fun together with your daughter. I'm not asking for a lifetime commitment. Not yet anyway. We'll take all the time we need."

Catherine lifted misty eyes to his. "But why, Jonah? Why me? Why my daughter? When so many other women out there would jump at the chance to spend time with you?"

He met her answer with a shrug of his broad shoulders. "I guess I just like being with you." *And God has led me back to you!*

"I find that hard to believe when there are so many desirable women available. I saw the way some of those beautiful women looked at you at the country club that night. Why not spend your time with them? I'm sure any one of them would be thrilled to date you. Why not them? It would certainly make your parents happy."

He slowly rose and began to pace about the room. "To be honest, Cat, I've played the field all these years—mostly looking for a woman to hang on my arm when I needed a date for one function or another, instead of for a wife. I never wanted to get serious with any of them. As I told you, after watching my parents' sham of a marriage, it was the last thing on my mind, especially to Alexandra. And my med school buddies' marriages? I won't even go there. You don't want to hear about those fiascos."

He hoped he was making sense, but even to his own ears his words didn't sound entirely plausible. "Actually, I haven't had time for women." He knelt down before her and captured her hands in his. "Then, thanks to the Lord, I found you again."

She frowned. "Me?"

He nodded. "Several years ago after my grandpa's funeral, my grandma told me how much she loved my grandpa and how she was going to miss him. I told her she could find another man to love. I think I was about twelve or thirteen at the time."

He scooted onto the sofa beside her and slid his arm around her shoulders, cradling her head against his chest. "Grandma said, 'Jonah, if you're fortunate enough to find a perfect love and you feel it's God's will for you to marry her, hold on to that love for as long as you can. Not everyone finds that kind of love.' Unfortunately I didn't listen to her advice." As his chin nuzzled her hair, he slid his other arm around her and whispered, "You were that love, Cat. The love my grandma was telling me about. I let you get away, and there's never been another. I see that now."

"But—"

"Shh. Let me hold you."

&

She gazed into his eyes. Somehow she had to distance herself from him. Something about this whole situation didn't ring true. But what was it? Was she being paranoid? Or was he being sincere in his words and actions toward her? Or was he simply doing what he thought she expected him to do?

Before she could rationalize any further, his lips sought hers. Despite her reticence, she could feel the tension in her body slipping away as their lips met. When they drew apart, she let out a nervous chuckle.

"What? Why are you laughing?"

"You've got cream all over your face!"

twelve

Catherine and Joy located a couple of empty seats on the bleachers behind home plate and sat down.

"It should be a good game. I know Sunni was sure revved up about it." Catherine shielded her eyes from the blazing sun and searched the field for her daughter.

"So Jonah said he'd be here, huh?"

"Yes."

"And you've decided to let him spend time with Sunni? After all the things you said to me?"

Catherine shrugged. "I hope I'm doing the right thing, but look at me. I've had an operation that would have cost who-knows-how-many dollars, and after ten years of agony my face is nearly back to normal. And what does he ask in return?"

"To spend time with you and your daughter! Doesn't that request seem a little strange to you? Wake up, Catherine. Smell the coffee. This is a man who probably has enough money to go out and buy himself a kid, if that's what he wants."

"Joy!"

"Well, he could. Oh, I don't mean actually buy, but he could adopt. Single people do it all the time these days. They'd probably even let me adopt a kid. As warped as I am!"

Catherine jabbed at her sister's arm. "Then why don't you? You like Sunni."

Joy frowned. "Are you kidding? Not all kids are like Sunni."

"That's exactly what Jonah said. They have so much in common, those two, and they're both sports nuts."

A shadow fell across them, and they turned to see Jonah standing over them. "Hi, Cat. Joy. Sure glad to see the game hasn't started yet. I didn't want to be late."

The two women scooted over and made room for him. He folded his long legs into the narrow space between the bleacher rows. "What's the holdup? Why aren't they starting?"

Joy searched the area. "I don't know. I don't see the coach anywhere, and the kids are just milling around."

Jonah stood and scanned the field. "Why don't I go ask Sunni what's happening? Excuse me, ladies. I'll be right back. Save my seat."

"Man, is that guy handsome," Joy said after a low whistle. "If I'd known he was going to grow up looking like that, I'd have gone after him myself. I could've replaced you easily since we look so much alike."

Catherine grinned. "But you don't have my sparkling personality."

Joy grew serious. "You mean the one you used to have before that night? You know, Catherine, your personality did change after that. You've been pretty low-key, but these past few days since that reconstruction I've seen the old you coming back. You're actually blossoming. I'm glad Jonah talked you into that operation."

"Me, too."

"I just hope it doesn't end up costing you more than you're prepared to pay. I'd hate to see you hurt again."

❧

Jonah located Sunni among the group of uniformed girls. "What's the holdup?"

She raised her brows. "I don't know. The other team's coach told us to wait because our coach wasn't here yet."

A man Jonah had never seen before crossed the field and stuck out his hand with a friendly smile. "Oh, good. I'm glad to see one of the fathers here. I just got a call on my cell phone from Coach Blevins. His car was broadsided. No one was hurt, but he won't be able to get here. He asked me to find one of the fathers and ask him to fill in as coach—just for today. Will you do it?"

Sunni grabbed Jonah by the hand. "Oh, please, please, please. Be our coach."

The child looked so cute and persuasive standing there in her softball uniform. *Why not?* Jonah asked himself. He was going to stay for the game anyway. Why not take over the coach's job for the afternoon? It might be fun. "Sure. Be happy to. What do I need to know?"

❧

Catherine stood and peered at the area near home plate. "What are they doing now?"

Joy joined her. "Where's Jonah?"

"Oh, there he is. He's walking toward the bench, and Sunni's team is with him, but I don't see their coach."

One of the mothers, who had also gone to check on the game, climbed back onto the bleachers and announced loudly, "The girls' coach had a car wreck, and one of the fathers has volunteered to take his place. The game will be starting in a few minutes."

Joy and Catherine smiled at one another and said in unison, "Jonah."

❧

"I'd say this calls for pizza!" Jonah yelled after Sunni's team batted in the winning score. "And it's on me!"

The players cheered and clapped their hands and crowded around him.

"Jonah! How are you going to take all these kids for pizza?" Catherine asked.

He pulled his cell phone from his pocket. "Easy. I'm going to order it. Would you and Joy gather all the kids and parents and get me a head count while I call the pizza place on the phone? I'll order drinks, too."

Joy's brows lifted. "What a man. I think you'd better grab

that guy after all. He's a rarity."

The pizza truck arrived a half hour later with a huge stack of hot pizzas and dozens of cold drinks. Jonah quieted the girls and prayed, and Catherine and Joy helped the temporary coach distribute everything.

"There's plenty for everyone," he assured the little girls swarming around him. "Remember—no trash lying around. We have to leave this field as clean as we found it. Everybody put your trash in the barrel over by the backstop when you're finished."

Joy nodded to her sister. "Environmentally correct, too. This guy's got it all."

Catherine nodded. "He sure does."

Joy chuckled. "All but you and Sunni, and I have a feeling you two are on his wish list."

"We've agreed neither of us is interested in a serious commitment, and we're not going to let our relationship go any further. We're only friends."

"Ha! I'll believe that when I see it. Lots of luck, Sis."

One of the mothers Catherine hadn't met yet came over to her after depositing hers and her daughter's trash in the big barrel. "Mrs. Barton?" The woman looked from one to the other, her face turning pink. "I don't know which of you is Mrs. Barton."

"I'm Mrs. Barton," Catherine said with a smile toward her sister.

"Well, Mrs. Barton, your husband is surrounded by those girls, and I can't seem to get to him. Would you please tell him how much we appreciate his filling in for the coach today? He did a marvelous job. And being such a Christian influence with his praying and all, I think the girls need to keep him. And the pizza! What a wonderful idea—and to think he paid for everything himself. Well, we think he's spectacular."

"But I—"

Joy nudged her in the ribs. "We'll tell him. I'm sure he'll be glad to hear it."

As the mother walked away, Catherine turned to her sister with a frown. "What was that nudge for?"

"Come on—be serious. I rescued you. Weren't you about to tell her Jonah wasn't your husband? Did you really want to have to explain to a stranger why he was here?"

"No. Of course not."

"See. As I said, I rescued you."

After the mess was cleaned up and everyone headed for their cars, Sunni asked if she could ride with Jonah. Catherine wanted that time with her daughter. She loved to share the after-game excitement of a win with her. But she also wanted Sunni to be happy. She gave her permission and watched her daughter and the tall, handsome man walk together to his car.

"How can I compete with that, Joy?" Catherine asked, stepping into her sister's old station wagon. "I'm losing her."

"Why do you have to compete?"

Catherine let out a long sigh. "She's my daughter, that's why. I can't begin to give her the things Jonah can. I know I shouldn't be jealous, but I am."

❧

Jonah pulled out of the parking lot and onto the busy street. He could hardly believe what had happened. He'd actually coached a bunch of ten-year-old girls and enjoyed every minute of it. In fact, he thought he could make a steady diet of it. He peeked at the pitcher seated beside him in her baseball cap and half wondered how much he'd have to pay their regular coach to let him finish out the season in his place.

"Hey, Flash. You were pretty good out there on that mound today. Do you realize how many players you struck out? And that homer you hit. You must have hit it right on the sweet spot."

Sunni wriggled her nose. "Sweet spot? What's a sweet spot?"

Jonah took his eyes off the road just long enough to catch another glimpse of his passenger. "That's the spot on the bat that makes the ball go the longest distance when you hit it."

She picked up her bat from the floor and twisted it around. "I don't see any sweet spot. Is there one on my bat?"

He grinned. "They don't mark it. You have to find it by trial and error."

The bat plopped back on the floor beside her glove.

"I'll help you. We'll find it. I think I can help you with your pitching, too. Not that you aren't doing great. You are, but I have a pointer or two that might come in handy."

He heard a big sigh. "What's the sigh for?"

She pulled her legs up onto the seat and folded them beneath her. "I was just wishing."

"Wishing? For what?"

"That I had a dad. Some of the girls thought you were going to be my dad since you came to my game. But I told them you were just a friend. It's not fair."

"I'm not your dad, but I will be your friend. And I'll come to your games. All of them. I'll get your schedule from your mom and mark them on my calendar at the clinic, so I won't forget."

She brightened. "Oh, would you? I like having you at my games. And thank you for the pizza. Everyone thought that was so kewl. It made me feel good."

He wheeled the car into the driveway and turned off the engine. "Pizza made you feel good?"

He gathered up her softball gear as she watched him. "Uh-huh. I think if I had a dad he would've ordered pizza for everyone, like you did."

He watched her struggle to the front door with her ball and bat and glove under one arm and her book bag under the other. How could buying a few pizzas and coaching a team of little girls make a guy feel like a king? he wondered.

❧

The next few weeks it seemed Jonah spent most of his free time at the Barton house. Between trips to the ice cream store, softball games, watching videos, and a myriad of other activities, he was there nearly every day. Sunni seemed to be loving every minute of it, but Catherine wasn't. Oh, in some ways she thought she was. But at times she felt shut out of her daughter's life. Where Sunni used to turn to her mother, she was now turning to Jonah, and it hurt.

Jonah seemed to have accepted their platonic status. He was warm and friendly and hadn't sought more since the day they'd made their agreement. Oh, he'd kissed her on the forehead several times and put his arm around her and given her little hugs—only not the kind of loving gestures she secretly wanted but wouldn't admit.

"I love you, Sunni," Catherine said one night as she closed the storybook and tucked the covers beneath her daughter's chin. "I know it hasn't been easy for you, not having a dad around. But I hope you realize, Honey, that I'm here for you. Anytime you need me. I love you, Baby. You're my life. I'd do anything humanly possible for you. Maybe even the impossible!"

Her daughter slipped an arm about her neck and pulled her down to her. "I know, Mom. I love you, too. You're the greatest. All my friends think so and say they wish their mothers were just like you. But I was wondering—why don't we go to church the way Dr. Shelton does?"

Taken aback by her question, Catherine kissed her daughter's cheek then released herself from her hug. "I know you're enjoying having Dr. Shelton in your life—"

"He's so nice, Mom. He says he's going to take me to—"

"I hope you're not becoming too attached to him," Catherine cautioned, cutting into her sentence. "Dr. Shelton's a busy man. He may not always be able to spend this kind of time with you. I just don't want to see you disappointed."

Sunni stretched and let out a big yawn. "Don't worry, Mom. He promised he'd be around as long as I need him. He likes me, and all my friends think he's really neat."

"I know he said that, but sometimes people say things they may mean at the time, only. . ." *How can I word this so she'll understand?* "I—I just don't want to see you get hurt, Sweetie." She wanted to say more, to warn her daughter about the dangers of becoming too dependent on Jonah, but it wouldn't do any good. Sunni was fast asleep.

❧

Ten candles burned brightly on the beautiful birthday cake Catherine had baked and Joy had decorated.

"Don't forget to make a wish, Honey."

"I already have," Sunni told her mother. She filled her lungs with air and blew all the candles out with one single blast. "I wished for a daddy."

The three adults looked at each other uncomfortably.

Jonah took the situation in hand. "You're a windy kid," he teased, tugging the girl back onto his lap and giving her a bear hug. "So you're ten years old today. Do you feel any older?"

Her mother watched in silence. Lately Sunni had rebelled when she'd tried to hug her, saying she was getting too old for such things. But she didn't seem to mind at all when Jonah hugged her. Catherine found herself filled with envy.

Sunni covered a giggle with her hands.

Jonah playfully pulled her hands away from her face. "You know, Sunni—I thought you were the only giggly girl around, until I started coaching your softball team. Now I know all girls your age are gigglers. And wigglers."

The birthday girl grinned.

"And guess what? I have a surprise!"

Sunni lifted her brow and beamed. "A birthday surprise?"

He shook his head. "Not exactly, but I think you'll like it. Or, at least, I hope you will. Coach Blevins called and asked if I'd take over as coach of your softball team for the rest of the season. Seems he's having some sort of family problems. And I said yes!"

Sunni shrieked, then jumped up and down and clapped her hands. "Oh, that is so kewl. Wait until I tell my friends!"

Catherine gulped hard. Coaching Sunni's team would bring him even closer to the girl. Things were spinning out of control, and she had no idea how to stop them. Only Joy seemed to notice her reaction to his news. The other two were chattering endlessly about Jonah's plans for the team.

"Hey, the ice cream's going to melt. You can talk softball later." Joy handed the knife to her niece. "Cut away, Kiddo. It's your birthday."

Sunni cut big wedges of cake and licked the sweet frosting off her fingers.

"Hey, go easy," her mother warned, handing her daughter a napkin. "Or there won't be room in that tummy of yours for ice cream."

The four enjoyed the ice cream and cake, then gathered around the coffee table to watch Sunni open her presents.

Catherine gave her new jeans, three knit shirts, a pair of summer sandals, a video game she'd been wanting, and a charm bracelet with her name engraved on it. Sunni "oohed" and "ahhed" over each gift as she opened it, much to her mother's delight.

Next came her aunt's gifts. A new softball glove, a pair of hiking boots, a lanyard with a whistle attached, and a new net for the basketball goal in the backyard to replace the torn one.

Sunni kissed her mother and her aunt and thanked them for the wonderful presents.

Jonah took her by the hand and pulled her down on the sofa next to him. "Aren't you wondering where my gift is?"

Sunni looked at him in surprise. "No. You've done so much for me already. I didn't expect one from you. Being my new coach is enough!"

"Well, I have one for you. But you know men. We don't wrap presents very well, so I left mine in the car. Sit right there, and I'll run out and get it."

As soon as he was out the door, Joy turned to her sister. "Wonder what he got for her?"

Catherine shrugged. "Something nice. Jonah doesn't do anything halfway."

The door opened, and he was back, holding something wrapped loosely in a bath towel.

Joy clapped her hands. "Oh, you bought her a set of towels for her bathroom. How thoughtful. Great gift for a ten year old."

Catherine put her hand over her sister's mouth. "Joy! Don't be facetious."

Sunni's eyes widened. "You didn't have to get me a present, Dr. Shelton. Really, you didn't."

He motioned toward the sofa, and they both sat down. "I guess, considering the crude wrappings, I should tell you to close your eyes and hold out your hands, but I won't. I don't want you to drop it."

Sunni giggled and nudged him in the ribs with her elbow.

Her mother flinched at her child's behavior. "Sunni!"

Jonah laughed. "It's okay. Sunni and I understand each other, don't we, Kid?"

She nodded.

"Open it," Jonah said, removing the towel from the plain brown box.

She pulled the tape off the box and lifted the lid. Inside was another box. She saw the picture on the box and gasped. "It's a laptop computer! Oh, Dr. Shelton, my very own computer. My friends don't even have their own computers!"

Catherine stepped over to her daughter's side and looked at the box. "Oh, Honey. That's way too expensive a gift for a child your age."

"No, it's not." Jonah helped the girl remove the computer from its packaging. "I want her to have it."

Sunni held up the computer for them all to see and beamed. "Will you teach me how to use it, Dr. Shelton?"

"Sure. With your mother being the computer whiz she is, you should pick it up in no time." He pulled the girl close and began showing her how to hook up the transformer.

Catherine grew quiet. She'd been saving her money this year so she could buy an inexpensive, no-frills computer for her daughter for Christmas. Now Jonah had given her a top-of-the-line laptop with all the bells and whistles. How could she expect to compete with a gift like that? The inexpensive presents she'd scrimped and saved for now paled beside his exorbitant gift.

"Guess he topped us, didn't he, Sis?" Joy whispered.

"He sure did," Catherine whispered back. "And I don't like it one bit."

Joy left soon afterward, and Catherine carried Sunni's gifts to her room while Jonah and the girl hovered over the new computer. She was feeling very left out of her daughter's life.

"Time for bed, Honey," she announced, faking a cheerful tone once the room had been tidied up. "Since all your friends are coming over for your birthday slumber party tomorrow night, you need to get your rest."

Sunni didn't move. Catherine was about to repeat herself when Jonah took the computer from Sunni's hands and placed it in his lap. "Your mom says it's your bedtime. I think we've done enough for one night. I—ah—your mother or I will help you more tomorrow."

The girl obediently headed for bed after thanking Jonah again.

Catherine shook her head and wished she had those same powers of gentle persuasion. Sunni was an obedient child, but rarely did she obey her that quickly.

Sunni called Jonah when she was ready for her bedtime story, but he suggested that since it was her birthday perhaps her mother should read it to her. Catherine jumped at the chance.

"Into bed with you," she told her daughter once she'd donned her pink nightshirt, the one with the words "One Kewl Kid" emblazoned in psychedelic colors across its front. She placed the huge stuffed teddy bear, the one she'd given Sunni for Christmas, in the bed beside her and pulled the pastel log-cabin quilt up about her slim shoulders. The one and only quilt she'd ever made. "I love you as—"

"I know! As high as the heavens, as deep as the oceans, and as wide as the universe," Sunni cut in, with the smile that always made Catherine's heart sing. "I love you, too, Mom. You're the greatest mom there ever was. And thanks for the birthday party and the terrific presents."

Remembering the expensive gift Jonah had given her, Catherine let out a sigh. "I wish I could have given you more, but—"

"Don't worry, Mom. It's okay. I loved the things you gave me, especially the jeans and the charm bracelet. They're really neat. I can hardly wait to show my friends that cute little teddy bear charm."

"I'm glad you like it, Sweetie. Each time you wear it, I hope you'll remember that I love you very, very much and you're my extra-special girl. I'm very proud of you." She kissed her daughter's cheek, picked up the book, and began to read.

Fifteen minutes later Catherine turned off the light and slipped out of her daughter's room. She felt much better about her relationship with Sunni. Jonah was nowhere in sight.

He must have gone home, she thought. *Oh, well. I'll wash up the cake and ice cream dishes in the morning and go on to bed early for a change.* She was turning out the living room lights when she heard a noise coming from the kitchen. She went to investigate and found Jonah, an apron tied around his waist, standing in front of the sink with his arms elbow deep in soap suds. He looked so domestic that it made her laugh.

He turned quickly. "What's so funny? Haven't you ever seen a man wash dishes?"

She stepped over beside him, pulled a clean towel from the drawer, and began drying the dishes he'd put in the rack to drain. "No, come to think of it—other than my dad on rare occasions—I never have."

He eyed her suspiciously. "Not even Jimmy?"

"Jimmy? No, not even him. He thought dishes were women's work."

"Well, if I were your husband, I'd help you with the dishes." He let the water out of the sink and wiped his hands on the hand towel.

"If you were my husband, I'd probably have a top-of-the-line stainless steel dishwasher and someone to load it!" she exclaimed and untied the apron from around his waist.

"I guarantee it!"

"That was some birthday present you gave Sunni," she said matter-of-factly. "Made mine and Joy's look like junk from the bargain basement."

He tapped her nose playfully. "Do I detect a note of sarcasm?"

"If you must know, yes. Jonah, I feel like I'm playing second fiddle around here. All I hear from morning to night is Dr. Shelton said this and Dr. Shelton did that. My own daughter barely acknowledges my existence anymore, and I'm getting a little sick of it." She couldn't believe how her anger had escalated with each word.

"I can't believe it! You're jealous!"

She stormed out of the room, flipped on the living room lights, and plopped herself onto the sofa. "You bet I am."

"I like being around her. She's a great kid," he said, following her into the living room.

"Well," she said with fire in her eyes, "if you like kids so much, why don't you marry Alexandra and have your own kids? Instead of trying to take over mine?" She was so angry, her head hurt.

"Cat, I've already told you. I don't love Alexandra!"

"Then marry someone else! I don't care who. Just go off and have your own kids! Sunni is mine, do you hear? She is not your child!"

Jonah took a deep breath before answering. "Look, Catherine. I love Sunni as much as if she were my own flesh-and-blood daughter. You've already agreed I can spend time with her."

"I've changed my mind," she snapped back.

"You can't change your mind."

"Oh, but I can. I just did! Leave us alone, Jonah. If you're so crazy about having a daughter, go find some woman who is willing and have your own!"

Jonah dropped onto the sofa, his head in his hands. "I can't have my own children, Catherine. I'm sterile!"

thirteen

"You—you're sterile?" The words exploded from her mouth. "You can't have children?"

He lifted his head slowly, his eyes filling with a sadness she'd never seen before. "Yes, the second year I was in med school I got the mumps, and well—you know what they can do to a man. I haven't been totally honest with you. It's one of the main reasons I've never married. Any woman I'd marry could never conceive a child, and that didn't seem fair. All that stuff about my not wanting kids—that's a bunch of boloney. I lied to you. I'd love to have kids of my own."

Catherine's heart clenched within her. "But what about Alexandra? You two were talking about marriage."

"I guess that's one reason I dated Alexandra, more than any of the others. She wasn't interested in marriage at first, and she never wanted kids. She hated the idea of going through a pregnancy and possibly ruining her perfect figure. Even the idea of adopting didn't appeal to her."

She gasped and jumped to her feet. Suddenly everything became clear. How could she have been so gullible? Since Jonah couldn't have children of his own, he'd decided he was going to use Sunni as a substitute daughter! She couldn't let that happen. It wasn't fair to Sunni or to her.

She backed away quickly and pointed her finger toward the door. "Get out of my house! I won't be part of your ridiculous scheme!"

"But, Cat—"

"She's mine! Mine! Do you hear me? Get out!"

Their gazes locked. Jonah moved toward her. She stepped

away from him and hurried to open the door.

"You're making a big mistake, Cat—"

"No," she retorted. "You're the one who's making a big mistake. Not me." Her voice shook with emotion. "I feel sorry for you, but I refuse to share my daughter with you."

He took hold of her arm. "I'm going to settle this once and for all, Catherine."

She tried to jerk away from his grasp. "Settle what, Jonah?"

He threw his free arm about her waist and pulled her so close she could see the anger in his eyes. "I don't care what you say. I think I'm Sunni's father. I'm going to demand a paternity test!"

⁂

The phone rang four times before Catherine reached over to answer it. All she could think about was the way Jonah had stormed out of her house after his earth-shaking announcement. Sleep had eluded her most of the night. She had risen early and slipped into her office as quietly as possible to avoid waking her daughter. A deep sigh escaped. She muttered, "Good morning. Hayley-Barton Web Design," in a near monotone.

"Hey, Sis, you sound weird. Where's that bubble I usually hear in your voice when I call?"

Catherine leaned back against the headrest of her office chair and closed her eyes. "My bubble burst, Joy. Jonah burst it big-time."

"How? I thought you two, or should I say three, were getting along famously."

She swallowed hard. "He still thinks he's Sunni's father."

Joy gasped. "Oh, great!"

"He's demanding a paternity test."

"Why? What happened?"

Catherine straightened in her chair. "He's sterile. That's the reason he's never married. Since he met Sunni, he's decided he wants to be a daddy."

"Oh, boy. How did that big decision happen to come about?"

"My big mouth, that's how. I confessed I was resentful of the time and attention and gifts he was heaping on my daughter, and I told him—"

"You told him what?"

"That I didn't want him around her anymore, and he accused me of being jealous."

"Are you?"

Catherine gnawed at her lower lip. "Yes, I guess I am. He got a little huffy about it, so I told him to go find a wife and have his own kids, if he wanted them so much. To leave my daughter alone. That's when he told me he couldn't have kids. He had the mumps in his early twenties." Her voice cracked slightly. "He's sterile."

"Tough," Joy said with sympathy in her voice. "So did you finally tell him to get lost?"

"Close to it. When I quit being little Miss Gullible, it suddenly dawned on me. Since he can no longer have children, and since he discovered Sunni's birth date, he's convinced himself she could be his. He says he's going to do whatever it takes to find the truth." The lump rising in her throat made it difficult to talk. "What am I going to do, Joy? I don't want Sunni to have to go through this."

"Have you talked to a lawyer?"

She nodded. "Yes, first thing this morning. He said Jonah had every right to demand the test, considering our one night together as husband and wife and Sunni's birth date."

"Bummer."

"Bummer is right. I don't—"

Joy broke in. "Do you still love him, Sis?"

Catherine closed her eyes then answered softly, "Yes, I guess I do."

"Then what's the trouble? Marry the guy, and you two can share her."

"Marry him? Are you crazy? He'd never go for that, and there are other problems. Monumental problems!"

"Like—?"

Catherine transferred the phone to her other hand and fingered the cord absentmindedly. "For one—he doesn't love me. I'd only be part of the package. And his parents hate me."

"So what're you going to do?"

She shrugged. "Nothing. My hands are tied. The next step is up to Jonah. I just hope he doesn't go through with this paternity test threat."

Catherine hung up the phone and tried to focus on the Webpage she was designing for her newest client, but it was impossible. She stood, stretched, and reached for the coffeepot to pour her fourth cup when the phone rang again. "Good morning. Hayley-Barton Web Design."

"I've made the arrangements. You need to have Sunni at the clinic at four o'clock this afternoon for blood tests."

She didn't have to ask who the caller was. The voice was all too familiar. "So you're going through with this?"

"Yes. We can do this the easy way, and you can cooperate, or I can get a court order. Either way, the test is going to be done, and there's nothing you can do to stop it. If you'd prefer another clinic do the test, that's fine with me."

She felt faint and grabbed the edge of her desk. "No. I—ah—yes—okay—I'll have her at your clinic right after school is out. But—"

"But what?" he asked gruffly.

She swallowed hard. "Please don't tell her why. Let's just let her think this is a routine checkup. Will you do that much for me? There's no need for her to know about any of this, Jonah. She's not your daughter. You'll find that out when the test results come back. Jimmy was her father."

There was a pause. "Of course. The last thing I want to do is hurt that little girl. I'll expect you both at four."

"How—how long will it be?" she stammered. "Until—"

"Several days. If you like, I'll make sure we both get the results at the same time."

"That'll be fine."

Sunni didn't seem to suspect anything out of the ordinary when Catherine picked her up after school and explained she was going for a general checkup.

Jonah met them at the door of his clinic, but he departed after introducing them to another doctor on his staff who would do the actual examination and draw the blood. To Catherine's relief, when they left the clinic she didn't see Jonah.

★

Jonah inserted the key in the front door of his parents' home with a heavy heart. How could things with Cat have become so messed up? He had no intention of trying to take Sunni away from her mother. He should have made that clear, but Cat was so indignant and sure of herself that it made him angry. But, angry or not, how could he have been so inconsiderate of her feelings? If their roles were reversed, he'd be every bit as upset as she was, and he knew it.

He dropped his keys on the hall table and started up the stairway to his room. Just then he heard his parents talking in the living room and decided to join them. He stopped at once when he heard his father's words. "What if the test proves our son is that child's father? I mean, if it does, Jonah may never speak to us again. I hope there's no way he'll ever find out we've robbed him of five years of her childhood."

"You wouldn't be talking about me and Catherine, would you, Father?" Jonah stepped into the room.

The elder Shelton shot a frantic look toward his wife.

"Ah—just how much did you hear, Son?"

"Enough."

His mother let out a little gasp and backed away. "We were only trying to protect you, Jonah. You were so young and in college—"

"When did you discover Catherine had a daughter?" His gaze shot from one parent to the other. A sickening feeling tugged at his stomach. He needed answers, and he wasn't going to be satisfied until he got them.

His father placed his hand on his son's shoulder, but Jonah shoved it away. "Now, Son, calm down. Let's discuss this rationally. No need to raise your voice."

"You've known about Sunni all these years, and you never told me?"

Horace Shelton cleared his throat nervously. "I was in Wichita on a business meeting about five years ago, and I happened to see her and that daughter of hers in a restaurant. One of those little birthday cakes restaurants provide was sitting on their table with five candles on it. I overheard that girl—"

"That girl's name happens to be Catherine, Dad. At least have the decency to call her by name."

"Catherine." The older man let out his breath. "I overheard Catherine wish her daughter a happy fifth birthday. Well, needless to say, I was stunned. If she was five at that time, there was a good chance she was your daughter. I told your mother when I returned home, and she agreed with me that we shouldn't tell you about it."

Jonah balled his fists, his anger rising. "You never even said hello to her?"

"I never talked to her. And she never saw me. I made sure of that."

Eldora Shelton nodded. "Your father and I spared you the trouble it would have caused you, if you'd thought you might have a daughter. You should be grateful."

"You spared me? What exactly did you spare me from? The joy of being Sunni's father?" He pounded his fist in his other hand. "Do you have any idea what you might have done to me? To Catherine? And to that precious little girl?"

His parents exchanged a questioning look. "We thought we were doing the right thing," his father said.

"Right thing? For whom? Certainly not me! Certainly not Sunni. That little girl may be your grandchild! Doesn't that knowledge do anything for you?"

His father shoved his hands into his pockets and looked away.

Jonah's palms came down on the coffee table with a thud. "Do you have any idea what your silence may have done to Sunni? And Catherine?" He ran his fingers through his hair. "I'm going to Catherine. I have no idea how I can ever make this up to her, but I'm going to try. And, for your information, Mother, Catherine is the only woman I've ever loved. And if she'll have me I am going to marry her!"

"Oh, Jonah, don't say that! You're not thinking clearly." His mother tried to reach out to him, but he stepped away.

"I've been a stupid, blind fool. I've been so focused on proving Sunni is my daughter that I've turned her mother against me. I don't care if I'm her father or not. It's Catherine I love. I'm going after her, and if she says yes she'll be Mrs. Jonah Shelton before this month is over. And this time you won't stop us!"

"No, Jonah. I forbid it!" his mother screamed at him. She crossed her arms and stomped her foot.

"I'll be back later to pick up my things. I'm moving out," Jonah declared over his shoulder, ignoring his mother and heading for the front door, slamming it firmly behind him.

He climbed into his car and headed across town. How could he have been so blind?

"God," he cried out as the car wove in and out of traffic, "help me! I want to serve You, Lord. Honest, I do. But I need You to show me what to do, and please help Cat see her need of You. Give me the right words to say and the right timing. I pray I haven't messed up things beyond repair."

Fifteen minutes later he was standing on Catherine's doorstep.

fourteen

When the bell sounded, Catherine walked toward the door with mixed emotions . Inside she was a bundle of nerves. In some ways her life was falling apart, the life she'd guarded so carefully for ten years. In other ways that life was just beginning, and she wanted to tell Jonah about the decision she'd made.

She stood and held the knob for a moment then opened the door. "Hello, Cat," Jonah said quietly. He brushed past her into the room. "We have some things to settle, and it'd probably be best if Sunni didn't hear our conversation. Is she here?"

She shook her head, then followed him into the living room. "She's spending the evening with Joy." She dropped onto the sofa with a sigh and hugged a pillow to her chest.

Jonah sat next to her, turned, and looked into her eyes. "I don't know how to do this other than to ask you straight out. Is Sunni my daughter?"

She stiffened. "No, you are not Sunni's father. Jimmy was. I've told you over and over. You'll know it for sure when that stupid paternity test comes back." She was weary of the whole situation.

"I think it's time to get everything out in the open, Cat." He gently pushed a lock of hair from her forehead, then tilted her chin upward. "Tell me about the scar. We both know it wasn't done by broken dishes. I've seen too many surgeries to believe a crazy story like that one. Why wouldn't you tell me the truth? Does it have anything to do with me? Is that why you've been so secretive about it?"

Catherine winced at his words. But what he said was true.

He had a right to hear the rest of the story. What she'd had to tell him would have to wait. "Okay, Jonah, you win." She took a deep breath and began.

"When I heard your parents' car drive off from the motel that night, I hurried out to catch you. I wanted to beg you one last time not to leave me. But the car was already pulling out of the parking lot. I couldn't let you go. I loved you too much. So I ran down that dusty road chasing their car until I couldn't run anymore."

"I didn't see you. I never looked back."

"I was sure you didn't. After catching my breath, I turned and started walking back." She paused, finding it more difficult to tell this than she'd imagined.

"A man with a T-shirt over his head darted out of the bushes and grabbed me. I was terrified. I knew what he was going to do to me. He put a knife to my throat and threatened to kill me if I didn't cooperate. I'd just lost you, and my life didn't mean anything to me, but I fought him with every ounce of strength I had left, despite his threats. He got really angry. I knew he was going to hurt me, but I wasn't strong enough to hold him off for long."

Jonah leaned his head against hers and pulled her tightly against him. So tightly she could feel the pounding of his heart.

"If only I'd known. Oh, Cat, no woman should have to face what you went through. No wonder you're so protective of Sunni."

She brushed away a flood of tears and swallowed at the lump in her throat, the memory of that night still so vivid she could taste it. She would never forget the fear she'd felt.

"He said he was warning me one last time—to stop struggling or he would use the knife on my face."

He gasped. "But you didn't stop, did you?"

"No, I fought him even harder. I kicked and scratched and did everything I could think to do. Finally, a car came down the street, and he panicked. He jabbed the tip of the knife into my cheek, just under my jawline, and ripped it up the side of my face and over my ear. He called me terrible names and shoved me to the ground. Then he ran off into the darkness."

"My poor, poor Cat. If only I'd been there with you! If only I'd known."

Catherine felt something moist fall onto her cheek. It was a tear. Jonah was crying, too. She could feel sobs racking his body as she rested her head on his chest.

"But—but you weren't there," she said, not because she wanted him to feel her pain, but because that was how it happened. "You'd left with your parents."

"Did the car stop?"

"Yes, the couple helped me back to our motel room and called an ambulance. They stayed until it came. I've never seen them again, but I will be forever grateful to those two people. I could have bled to death if they hadn't come along when they did. I was so weak that I barely remembered what happened."

"Oh, Cat. Dear, dear Cat. What can I say? What can I do?"

She patted his hand. "Nothing, Jonah. It all happened a long time ago. You've helped rectify it. You've fixed my face."

He kissed the still-reddened evidence of the recent surgery. "I'm glad you finally let me do it, but I had no idea of what—"

She cupped his chin with her hand. "Don't blame yourself. You couldn't have known it was going to happen. I was in the wrong place at the wrong time."

He swallowed hard. "But I do blame myself, Cat. I do. I should have been there for you. Did they catch the guy?"

She shook her head sadly. "No. They never did. I don't know what I would have done without Joy. My parents fell apart when they saw me in the hospital, but Joy stayed by my side. And Jimmy was a rock."

Jonah stiffened. "Jimmy?"

She frowned. "Yes, Jimmy. He came to the hospital all

three days they kept me. He even paid my bill since my dad didn't have any hospitalization or insurance coverage. I felt like ending my life every time I looked in the mirror. Jimmy was a couple of years older than I was and had accepted a job in Wichita. He was leaving that next week. We'd been good friends at the shop where we both worked."

"I'm glad he was there for you. Sounds like he was a really nice guy."

"He was. When I told him what had happened between us—you and me—he offered to take me with him. He said we could be married, and he would take good care of me. Everyone in the beauty shop knew he'd had a crush on me."

"You accepted his proposal? Just like that?"

She shrugged. "What did I have to lose? You were gone. Our marriage had been annulled. Your parents had seen to that immediately. I didn't have money for college or any skills to get a good job. So I married him as soon as we got to Wichita."

Jonah's right fist slammed into his left palm. "That's why there wasn't a record of your marriage license in the Dallas newspapers!"

"You checked?" She was amazed that he would do such a thing.

"I was so sure you made up that story about Jimmy to cover the fact that I was Sunni's father."

"I wasn't lying to you, Jonah. He was a good man, and I loved him. *I* nearly died when he died. He'd been there every time I'd needed him, and he'd asked so little of me."

"And all this time I've been so sure Sunni was mine. I wanted her to be mine!"

She reached over to stroke his cheek. "I have to admit I wouldn't have been disappointed if I had been carrying your child after those few hours together on our wedding night. Somehow I would've managed. I loved you, Jonah." Her finger lightly traced his furrowed brows to ease his tension.

He lifted his hand to cup her face. "I'm glad we have this out in the open. No more secrets, okay?"

"There's one more thing I have to tell you."

He braced himself. "Oh, now what? Out with it. I think I can face anything after what we've been through."

Her eyes sparkled through her moist lashes. "I think you'll like this one."

"What?"

"I had a terrible time falling asleep last night. By two o'clock I was still wide awake. I wandered into the kitchen to get a drink of water, and as I came back through the living room I decided to turn on the TV, maybe check out CNN. But in the darkness I must've hit the wrong buttons on the remote, and some man was singing 'Amazing Grace.' I remembered my aunt singing that song when I was a kid, so I stopped to listen. When he finished, Billy Graham began to preach. I started to flip to another station, but something compelled me to watch."

&

Jonah had to bite his tongue to keep from shouting *alleluia!*

"I listened to the entire message, and for the first time I understood what you've been trying to tell me. God does love me! Despite all the dreadful things that have happened to me. I realized I'm a sinner, not just a victim. I listened to him explain how God sent His only Son so that through Jesus we can come to God and turn our lives over to Him, assuring us of eternal life with Him."

Jonah could stand it no longer. "God does love you, Cat. He loves all of us. We just have to receive that love and ask His forgiveness—and believe He's forgiven us."

"I did it, Jonah! I asked him, just like Billy Graham said. Right here in my living room, I turned my life over to Him. Suddenly everything you've said made sense. I've been so anxious to tell you. I knew you'd be pleased. You've been so patient with me."

Jonah pulled back, alarmed. He looked at her. "You're not

saying this because it's something you think I want to hear, are you? To appease me?"

Her eyes widened. "No! I would never do that! I've been so angry with God all these years. I thought He'd forsaken me. Now I realize it's just the opposite. He was here all the time. I'm the one who left Him! I see that now." Her chin dropped to her chest. "I always had a hard time believing He could forgive me. Now I know through Jesus He forgave me a long time ago, but I never accepted that forgiveness as mine."

"Look. I'm just a baby at this thing myself, Cat. I read my Bible every day now, but there is so much I don't know. But one thing I do know—His forgiveness is there, but we have to ask Him for it."

She nodded. "I have so much to learn. And I want my daughter to learn about God's Word, too. Children these days need all the help they can get." She smiled faintly. "I–I hope I'm not too late."

Jonah gave her a reassuring squeeze. "With God it's never too late."

She let out a sigh. "Somehow I knew you'd say that."

"I have a bit of news myself. I had quite a talk with my parents a couple of hours ago. I told them you were the only woman I've ever loved."

"You told them that? Why? What about Alexandra?"

Something in Jonah stirred as he held her and looked into her eyes, an emotion he hadn't felt since his teenage years. "I've already told you she means nothing to me. She was just a convenient companion who accompanied me when I attended social functions. That's all. I'd never marry her. Even if I hadn't found you." He pulled her close and nuzzled his face in her hair. "You know what else I told them?"

She cuddled against him. "No. What?"

He emitted a soft chuckle. "I told them that if you'd have me I'd marry you."

She straightened in his arms and searched his face. "You said that? Why?"

Jonah decided it was time to unburden his heart, too. "Because I would. I've never stopped loving you. Even when I heard you were married to someone else."

She smiled and touched the dimple in his cheek with her fingertip, as she had when they were young. "You'd better not ask me. I might say yes. Then what would you do?"

He smiled back, then bent and kissed her on the lips. He had everything life could offer, except for the two most important things a man could have. A wife he loved dearly, and children.

"Let's find out what would happen if I asked you to marry me," he said, grinning. He released his hold on her and dropped onto one knee. "I love you, Catherine Hayley-Barton," he whispered softly, gazing up into her misty eyes. "I love you so much that I'd do anything for another chance. And if you give me that chance I promise I'll never leave you again."

જ

Catherine's breath caught in her throat. Was she dreaming? Was this moment really happening?

"Will you marry me? Will you let me love you and take care of you and Sunni for the rest of our lives?"

She smiled through her tears. "Are you serious? Do you really mean this?"

"I've never been more serious. Will you?" He continued to kneel before her, his hands holding hers.

Catherine leaned over and kissed him. "Yes, dearest Jonah, I'll marry you. If you promise me this time it's for keeps."

જ

The next day Catherine met Jonah in his office at the appointed time. He had an envelope in his hands, the one with the long-awaited test results.

He kissed her tenderly, then took her hand in his and gave

it an affectionate squeeze. "I've thought a lot about Sunni. I know it's hard to believe, but the minute I met that girl I fell in love with her."

He paused thoughtfully, then held up the envelope between them. For a tense moment they stared at it, lost in their own thoughts.

"Cat, I want you to know," Jonah said, desperate to convince Catherine of his true feelings, "that even though we both know what these test results will say—that I'm not Sunni's biological father—you have to believe I'll love her as much as I would if she were my own flesh and blood."

She stood on tiptoes, kissed his cheek, and smiled at him. "I do believe it. I've seen the two of you together and the way you've treated her. Your love for her has been obvious. And I know she loves you."

He pulled her into his arms again and held her close. "But do you think she'll accept me as her dad? Not just as a friend?"

"Of course she will. You're everything she's ever wanted in a father. Remember her birthday wish?"

He blinked hard. "Of course I do. It nearly broke my heart."

"Mine, too," she whispered.

He smiled. "I say let's tear up the results. We already know what they're going to say." He held it out to her. "You make the first rip."

Slowly Catherine took the envelope from his hand. "You're sure? You don't even want to take a peek?"

He shook his head. "Not even a little one."

She yanked the envelope in half and handed it back to him. "It's still not too late."

Without a word he tore it in half again and placed it in the small metal wastebasket beside the desk. He pulled a book of matches from the top drawer, opened the flap, and tore off a single match. "I'm ready to end this once and for all. How about you?"

Catherine locked her arm in his. "Light the match."

Jonah lit the match, let it burn for a second, then ceremoniously dropped it into the wastebasket on top of the torn envelope and its contents.

"You're stuck with me now, Cat." He hugged her tightly to him while they watched the paper curl, burn, and turn to ashes.

His gaze caressed her lovely face, now free of the scar. The adoring face he'd loved for ten long years. The face of the wife he'd turned his back on at his parents' insistence. The woman with whom he would spend the rest of his life.

Jonah drew her close and kissed her like he'd wanted to kiss her from the moment she'd opened the door of her home and allowed him to come in. "I'll never again let you get away from me, Cat. We've lost so much precious time. Promise you'll stay with me always."

"I'm right where I want to be, Sweetheart." Her eyes shone. "You couldn't get rid of me if you tried."

Jonah kissed her once more then lifted his gaze heavenward. *Thank You, Lord. Only You could have worked this out. I've been so foolish. Only You could have given me back the love of a lifetime. Make me worthy of Catherine's love. Make me the husband You would have me to be. And please, God, help me be the kind of father Sunni deserves.*

"I love you, Jonah. I will always love you. We are meant to be together, my love. I know that now."

"I love you, too, Cat. I can't begin to tell you how much. You're the answer to my prayers. Let's go tell Sunni her birthday wish is about to come true. She's going to have a father!"

A Letter To Our Readers

Dear Reader:

In order that we might better contribute to your reading enjoyment, we would appreciate your taking a few minutes to respond to the following questions. We welcome your comments and read each form and letter we receive. When completed, please return to the following:

Fiction Editor
Heartsong Presents
PO Box 719
Uhrichsville, Ohio 44683

1. Did you enjoy reading *The Birthday Wish* by Joyce Livingston?
❏ Very much! I would like to see more books by this author!
❏ Moderately. I would have enjoyed it more if

_____

_____

_____

2. Are you a member of **Heartsong Presents**? ❏ Yes ❏ No
If no, where did you purchase this book? _____

_____

3. How would you rate, on a scale from 1 (poor) to 5 (superior), the cover design? _____

4. On a scale from 1 (poor) to 10 (superior), please rate the following elements.

____ Heroine   ____ Plot
____ Hero   ____ Inspirational theme
____ Setting   ____ Secondary characters

5. These characters were special because?_____

_____

_____

6. How has this book inspired your life?_____

_____

_____

7. What settings would you like to see covered in future
   Heartsong Presents books? _____

_____

_____

8. What are some inspirational themes you would like to see
   treated in future books? _____

_____

_____

9. Would you be interested in reading other **Heartsong
   Presents** titles? ❑ Yes   ❑ No

10. Please check your age range:
    ❑ Under 18   ❑ 18-24
    ❑ 25-34   ❑ 35-45
    ❑ 46-55   ❑ Over 55

Name_____

Occupation _____

Address _____

City_____ State_____ Zip_____

From Italy, with Love

4 stories in 1

$\mathcal{M}$otivated by letters, four women travel to Italian cities and find love. Four American women are compelled to explore the historic country that their parents and grandparents called "home"—along the way finding God's plan for themselves. Authors include: Gail Gaymer Martin, DiAnn Mills, Melanie Panagiotopoulos, and Lois Richer.

Contempoary, paperback, 352 pages, 5 $^{3}/_{16}$"x 8"

♥ ♥ ♥ ♥ ♥ ♥ ♥ ♥ ♥ ♥ ♥ ♥ ♥ ♥ ♥ ♥

Please send me _____ copies of *From Italy, with Love* I am enclosing \$6.97 for each. (Please add \$2.00 to cover postage and handling per order. OH add 7% tax.)

Send check or money order, no cash or C.O.D.s please.

Name _____

Address _____

City, State, Zip _____

To place a credit card order, call 1-800-847-8270.
Send to: Heartsong Presents Reader Service, PO Box 721, Uhrichsville, OH 44683

♥ ♥ ♥ ♥ ♥ ♥ ♥ ♥ ♥ ♥ ♥ ♥ ♥ ♥ ♥ ♥

Presents